LITERARY OUTLAW

A PULP FICTION MAGAZINE | ISSUE #1

IN THIS ISSUE:

WINDHAM REX........................... 3
John Graves

THE PARABLE OF THE SOWER 19
Kevin G. Summers

2 B R 0 2 B 29
Kurt Vonnegut, Jr.

DANCE MACABRE 35
Author Unkown

THE REPAIRER OF REPUTATIONS 41
Robert W. Chambers

WHO'S WHO 66
Author Unkown

THE BRIDGE OF SAN LUIS REY 73
Thornton Wilder

GONE 93
Patty Summers

BERENICE 94
Edgar Allan Poe

LITERARY OUTLAW #1
Copyright © 2024 by LiteraryOutlawLLC

Front Cover art by Vivid Covers
Back Cover photo by Joel Baldwin | Public Domain. Originally published in *LOOK Magazine, 1969*
Windham Rex | Copyright © 2024 by LiteraryOutlawLLC
The Parable of the Sower | Copyright © 2024 by Kevin G. Summers & James Hale
2 B R 0 2 B | Public Domain. Originally published in *If: Worlds of Science Fiction, January 1962*
Dance Macabre | Public Domain. Originally published in *Nightmare #1*
The Repairer Of Reputations | Public Domain. Originally published in *The King in Yellow, 1895*
Illustration on Page 42 | Copyright © 2011 by Tucker Sherry / AmazingMoondog. Used by permission.
Who's Who | Public Domain. Originally published in *Black Cat Comics #1*
The Bridge of San Luis Rey | Public Domain. Originally published in 1927
Gone | Copyright © 2003 by Patty Summers
Berenice | Public Domain. Originally published in *Scream #7*

The stories in this magazine are works of fiction. Names, characters, businesses, places, events and incidents are either the products of the author's imagination or used in a fictitious manner. Any resemblance to actual persons, living or dead, or actual events is purely coincidental.

All rights reserved. This book or any portion thereof may not be reproduced or used in any manner whatsoever without the express written permission of the publisher except for the use of brief quotations in a book review.

www.literaryoutlaw.com

WINDHAM REX

BY JOHN GRAVES

2992. THE DISTRESS CALL ARRIVED three days ago, when the starship *Gilead* was all the way on the other side of her barony. She was orbiting Oriza, and the crew was enjoying a bit of shore leave, when Governor Morrison's message reached the great old ship.

"Avalon has been attacked by reavers. It's... it's bad. A lot of men are dead, but the worst part... they took our children. Please, I know things haven't been good between us since your father passed away, since... I'm begging you, Captain Manthus, please help us."

Passed away.

Was that what you called it when a bunch of religious fanatics blew themselves up and took your father along with them? Windham Manthus had been dealing with the emptiness of his father's sudden death ever since, trying to fill up that hole with work, but the void was infinite and the work felt meaningless even in the best of times. Restock the ship... broker a settlement between two disparate worlds... monitor the Affiliation just in case they decide to invade the outer baronies... he had been trained for this life, but something about it left Windham feeling unsettled—unsatisfied.

Governor Morrison wasn't one of those born politicians—soft and fanatical without ever having done an honest day's work in their lives. He was well muscled under a sensible suit, and his skin was perpetually tanned from years of working in the sun. Morrison had suspended a decades-old agreement with *Gilead* when Windham's father was killed and began negotiations with the starship *Jericho*, which operated in an adjacent barony. It was treachery, plain and simple, and the two starships had nearly come to blows over the situation a number of times since Windham had taken over his father's command. Apparently *Jericho* wasn't doing such a good job of protecting the colony on Cheron-4 if reavers were landing on the planet and kidnapping children.

Windham had half a mind to let Governor Morrison and the people of Avalon lie in the bed they had made, but the thought of those poor children in the hands of space pirates was just too much for the young captain. Whatever their parents and democratically elected officials had done, those children were innocent and didn't deserve the lives of slavery and prostitution that lay before them if their present situation wasn't corrected immediately. Windham had been coming to Cheron-4 since he was a child himself, and even though the governor had broken off the old treaty, Manthus still felt a measure of responsibility for these people who had once been under his protection. He couldn't just stand by and let this happen. And so he gave the order to recall the crew and head toward Cheron-4 at top speed.

The governor's palace in Avalon wasn't much to look at. It was adequate, functional, perhaps even extravagant compared to the other buildings in town, but it was just brick and wood, with a copper roof slowly turning green in the elements. Windham had been to Elden-2, the jewel of the outer baronies, and Avalon paled in comparison. Still, there was something about this agrarian outpost that spoke to him. If fate had dealt him a different set of cards, he could see himself living out his life on a world like this. Milking cows and slaughtering hogs and never worrying about interstellar politics or if his crew was going to mutiny and put a knife in his back. There was a certain appeal to simplicity, but things hadn't worked out like that, and so he entered the governor's palace as the captain of the starship *Gilead*, and the guards stood at attention as he passed through the doors.

Charles Morrison was in his office when Windham arrived. His face was a mask of desperation as he stood and extended a hand over his desk. Windham took the governor's hand and they shook heartily. Could the damage that had been done between Avalon and *Gilead* be repaired? The captain hoped that the answer was yes.

Once the formalities were out of the way, they got down to business.

"What happened here?" Windham asked. "In your distress call you mentioned reavers..."

Morrison's eyes went dark. "I made the mistake of believing that Captain Gaines would have *Jericho* here in a heartbeat at the first sign of trouble, but when the shit hit the fan they were nowhere to be found."

Windham tried not to look too smug at this acknowledgment. After the collapse of the Planetary Union, most of the colonized systems were broken up into baronies under the protection of various starships or small fleets. The inner baronies, those closest to Earth, were endlessly trying to reestablish the republic they had lost, but the universe had seemingly moved on. In the outer baronies, however, human civilization was practically medieval. *Gilead* was ruled by a monarch whose pedigree stretched back nearly five hundred years. Things were much the same on the starship *Jericho*, and the two huge city ships had been both allies and enemies over the centuries. Right now, things weren't good between them, and while Windham would never rejoice over a bunch of kids being kidnapped and sold into slavery, he couldn't help but recognize this opportunity to restore Cheron-4 to *Gilead*'s barony.

"Space is vast," said the young captain. "It took *Gilead* three days to get here once we received your call, and *Jericho* is even farther away."

The governor nodded somberly. "Our children have been gone now for almost a week, and I fear..." His voice cracked, and Windham sensed that Morrison was not simply expressing the worries of a politician whose job was on the line.

"My own daughter, Eowyn, was also taken during the raid. She..." he paused for a long moment, his mind no doubt going to the dark places where fear and hopelessness feed on a man's soul. "They're out there somewhere, and who knows what those reaver bastards are doing to them. It's my fault, Captain Manthus. I never should have renounced our treaty."

He could have rubbed salt in that wound, but Windham could see that this man was already on the brink of despair. All of the other parents in Avalon were likely feeling the same thing right now, and Charles Morrison needed to be strong for them. "We'll find your children," Windham said, "all of them. And I'll bring you back the head of the man who orchestrated this crime."

The governor stared at him, a storm of fear swirling behind his eyes. "Thank you, sai. You give me hope."

Windham excused himself and headed toward the gateway that would take him back to his ship. He was tall and dark-haired and handsome in the prime of his life. At twenty-four years old and without the burden of a family to weigh him down, he was able to boldly make such a promise to this politician whose extended family had ruled Avalon since the colony was established about a century before. Windham knew that he would either deliver on his promise or die trying. But what of *Gilead*, the floating city that had been his family's birthright for generations? Windham had no wife to love him in the cold darkness of space, and no heir to assume the throne once he closed his eyes forever. There had been women in his life, of course, but not love and not even a marriage to strengthen alliances. And now with his father's body moldering in *Gilead's* crypt along with the bodies of his ancestors, Windham felt alone in the universe. He could

empathize with Charles Morrison, but he was incapable of understanding the man's terrible fear.

But he would know it soon enough.

WINDHAM STEPPED THROUGH A PORTAL in Avalon and emerged on the bridge of his starship. *Gilead* was enormous—built by the old United Planetary Federation back in 2599, she could accommodate fifteen thousand people on a sustained basis, and twenty thousand in a crisis situation. Her current complement, however, was only a little over seven thousand—men, women, and children.

"Captain on deck," said Grayson Ward, Windham's first mate. He stood at attention in an ancient show of respect. Ward was an older man, as smart as a fox and tougher than a cheap steak. Windham had looked up to Ward since he was a kid, and he truly didn't know how he would run this ship without the old man's advice and assistance.

"At ease." Windham took his place on the carved ironwood throne. A digital map of the stars spread over the walls and ceiling of the room. The captain studied the twinkling lights for a moment as he searched the night for his quarry. The reavers were out there somewhere, and with them, hopefully, the lost children of Cheron-4.

"I took the liberty of scanning for warp signatures," Grayson said. "From what I can tell, the reavers came and went on a single ship and headed toward the Chibok system."

"Chibok?"

"The black market of the galaxy. Aye, if those poor kids get split up, we'll never find them all." The first mate looked somber as he considered the possibility. His own son was only eighteen and just entering the service of his ship. Windham liked the lad, though it was hard to picture young Harrison taking over his father's job someday.

"It's possible that they're trying to throw us off their trail," said the captain. "Maybe they're heading toward Chibok and then diverting to some other port."

"Sir, with all due respect, while it's possible, it's not likely. Cheron-4 has been under *Jericho*'s protection for some time now, and I wouldn't be surprised if those bastards knew about the reaver attack and just looked the other way."

Windham scowled. He felt a deep responsibility for the people of Avalon, even though they had turned their backs on *Gilead*. He figured that his sense of responsibility might get him killed someday, just like his father. But if death came today or years down the line, he would follow where his duty led him, and right now it was leading him to Chibok. "Scour the Net, see if you can find anything..."

"I already have." Ward grinned. "Captain Wyatt of the starship *Saladin* is hosting a slave auction tomorrow evening at Chibok Station. He's been publicizing it all over the Dark Net. Unless this is some kind of trap, I believe we've found our missing children."

"Good work," said the captain. "Cloak the ship and proceed to the Chibok system at maximum warp.

We're going to make sure those reavers never forget the name *Gilead*."

THEY COULDN'T SIMPLY STORM ONTO Chibok Station with disruptors blazing and hope to free two hundred and seventy-six children. As much as Windham would have liked to kill every reaver responsible for this abomination, not to mention everyone who had traveled the stars in hopes of purchasing a slave, he knew that they needed a plan if they wanted any chance of returning those kids to their families.

Gilead had been policing this barony for centuries, and had captured a number of smaller vessels that could be of use in a situation such as this. Windham had one starship in mind—a light cruiser called the *Asuka* was dry-docked in one of the great ship's hangars. With a capacity of twenty-five, the *Asuka* was the perfect size to sneak up to Chibok Station and infiltrate the auction. *Gilead*, meanwhile, could remain cloaked until it was time to spring the trap.

"Are you sure you want to do this?" Ward asked for probably the fiftieth time. The rest of the away team was already on board the *Asuka* and awaiting their captain so they could depart. *Gilead* had dropped out of warp some distance from Chibok, well out of the station's sensor range, but the longer they waited here the more likely they were to get noticed.

"I'm sure," Windham said.

"I doubt that Captain Gaines would put himself in the middle of the action like you're about to do."

"Captain Gaines is a son of a bitch, and I'll do what I think is right. In this situation, I'm going to lead the away mission while you stay here and command *Gilead*."

His first mate chuckled. "You sound more like Captain Lightoller."

Windham couldn't help but smile. He had grown up on legends of William Lightoller and the adventures of the starship *Jerusalem*. Lightoller was well known for taking risks that always seemed to pay off in the end. "I hope I have a bit of the old boy's luck on this mission."

"I can't say that I'm thrilled, but there's no use trying to argue with you once your mind is made up. You're as stubborn as your father in that regard."

"You're not the first person to tell me that."

"And likely not the last, either."

"How's my disguise?" Windham touched the fake beard that was his only protection on this jaunt. The auction noticed made it clear that no weapons or armor were allowed on Chibok, which certainly meant that the crew of the *Saladin* would be armed to the teeth and everyone else would be totally vulnerable. Windham's face was instantly recognizable in this region of space, but the beard was hopefully enough for him to hide in plain sight, at least for a little while.

Hopefully.

"Looks good on you. You should keep it."

"I don't know about that."

"Go get those kids, Windham, I'll keep your seat warm."

"Good luck, Grayson."

They shook hands and then Windham boarded the *Asuka*. She launched from *Gilead*'s hangar and then immediately went to warp. Chibok was only a few hours away, and they were set to arrive just before the auction began. As Windham sat on the small ship's bridge, he prayed that this desperate plan would work.

"UNKNOWN VESSEL, IDENTIFY YOURself."

Windham didn't recognize the face on the *Asuka*'s view screen, but he assumed that this was one of the *Saladin*'s crew. He was ornately groomed with a set of glorious mustaches.

"I'm Captain Thawne of the starship *Asuka*."

"State your business."

"I'm here for the auction."

The reaver stroked his mustaches as he tapped a few commands on his computer console. "I'm transmitting the gateway code for the station. This code is unique, and once you've used it, it will change."

"How am I supposed to get off the station after the auction?"

"We'll give ye another code, cully."

The gateways were a series of networked portals that enabled people to pass through tremendous distances as easily as stepping through a door. The passcode would give Windham access to the station, but it would also give *Gilead*'s tinkers an entry point into Chibok Station's computer. If God was on their side, they could hijack the gateway network and have full access to the station.

Windham's computer dinged, indicating a new message had arrived. He checked the message and found an elaborate string of numbers and letters—the passcode.

"The auction's about to start. There be some pretty girls up for sale, let me tell ye. Better get on over there if ye want yer pick o' the lot."

"On my way," said Windham. "I can't wait."

Men like this had been stealing the weak and vulnerable for thousands of years and forcing them into lives of slavery and prostitution. Even in the ages when mankind considered himself to be enlightened, he was never more than a recession away from devolving into a Neanderthal. Windham had read about many of the famed captains of the old Union who had dealt in this sort of trade on the side. Some modern scholars even said that Captain Lightoller himself had kept a comfort woman, but Windham refused to believe it. He wanted to see his heroes as heroes, not mere mortals who could fall prey to temptation just like everyone else. People would never change, no matter how far their technology advanced. The strong would always prey on the weak, and the weak would always need someone like Windham Manthus to come along and set them free. There would be blood shed tonight, and if Windham had his way, every single reaver on the *Saladin* would be dead before *Gilead* left this system.

Another ding indicated a new incoming transmission. Windham

pressed a button and Grayson Ward's face appeared on the view screen.

"We've got access. Let's get this show on the road."

"Yes, sai," said Windham. He smiled sardonically.

THE PORTAL HUMMED TO LIFE ON THE *Asuka*, revealing a garishly-colored room on the other side of the doorway. There were dozens of people on the other side—most dressed in civilian clothes and a few here and there in red battle armor. These were the crew of the *Saladin*. The auction announcement had stated emphatically that no one was allowed to bring any sort of weapon on board Chibok station, and it appeared that the Wyatt's men were strictly enforcing this rule. There was a walkthrough scanner built into the Chibok side of the portal. If he tried to smuggle something on board the station, he would get caught and then get dead. So, armed with nothing but his cunning, Windham crossed the threshold, stepping from the bridge of the *Asuka* onto Chibok Station as easily as stepping from one room to another.

An armored guard stood on the other side of the gateway with a disruptor aimed right at the portal. His red battle armor looked weathered, as if it had seen plenty of use. There was a white skull painted on the reaver's breastplate, and he wore a helmet that hid his face behind a black visor.

"You're clear," he said in an amplified voice after examining the captain's scan.

Windham nodded as he walked past the armed guard and into the den of thieves. Chibok Station was notorious through this region of known space, but the captain had never been here in all of his twenty-some years. The system was located in the neutral zone between Affiliation space and the outer baronies. If Windham was correct about the history, this station was originally built as an ore-processing facility back when the United Planetary Federation ruled the galaxy. After the Galactic Civil War toppled the Union, the station had been abandoned and the rats and pirates moved in. Everything was painted like a whorehouse on Saturday night; it hurt Windham's eyes to look at it. He pressed through the crowd, trying to get as close as he could to the platform stage on the far side of the room.

A gigantic man in red armor stepped to the center of the stage. He wore no helm, and his dark hair and beard flowed over his armor in the most ostentatious way possible. He had half a dozen braids in his long beard, and twice as many in his hair. He might have seemed like a dandy if not for his pirate armor. Windham recognized him at once as Braedon Wyatt, captain of the starship *Saladin* and the most notorious reaver in known space.

"Gentlemen," said Wyatt, "it is truly a pleasure to make your acquaintance. I want to thank you profusely for attending this little shindig, it means ever so much to me and my crew."

The men in the crowd looked at each other uncomfortably, not sure if they should applaud or what. The tension in the room was thick, and

Windham felt particularly vulnerable without his gear. The reavers had set up this situation in order to give themselves a distinct advantage. It was smart business for sure, but it made him uncomfortable as hell.

"I know why you're all here, you devils, so let's get this auction under way, shall we?"

Wyatt grinned wolfishly as two of his men dragged a terrified girl onto the stage. She was older than Windham had expected—could be anywhere from seventeen to twenty—but the terror on her face made her look younger. He supposed that she could still be called a child, Governor Morrison had done just that, but it seemed like a stretch. The reaver leaned in toward the girl's ear and spoke softly, though his amplified voice was heard throughout the room.

"Take it off."

"Please, no..."

Wyatt brandished a taser at the girl—blue electricity flickered from the end of the weapon and the child began to whimper. "Take it off now."

The girl undressed in shame. She had long, brown hair with just a hint of wave to it, and her arms were brown from days spent working in the sun. She had a farmer's tan, and was pale everywhere else.

"Ain't she a lovely specimen?" Wyatt asked the crowd of gathered men, men who had come to purchase the flesh of another living person. "I know most of you probably are here for the younger ones, and we have those in plenty, but there must be a few of you out there that would enjoy the pleasures of this pretty little thing. Am I wrong?"

There crowd hooted and hollered like a bunch of horny men at a strip show. But this poor girl wasn't shaking it for a few credits, she was trembling all over, trying to cover herself with her hands and her hair. It made Windham sick, and the only thing he wanted more than to kill everyone in this room was to cover the poor girl. She looked up, and for a moment their eyes met. She had no way of knowing that he was here to rescue her—she must have thought that he was just another monster leering at her and trying to decide if this was the one he wanted to bid on. The girl looked away, ashamed.

"Let's start the bidding at—"

The crack of disruptor fire echoed in the distant corridors of the space station. Angry voices shouted unintelligibly. As the reaver captain paused, mid-sentence, Windham received a transmission in his earpiece.

"We've engaged the enemy," said Hollis Garner, one of *Gilead's* most promising rangers.

"It seems one of you wasn't entirely honest about his intentions here," said Wyatt. The reaver captain replaced the taser on his utility belt and drew a disruptor pistol in its place. He grabbed the naked farm girl around the waist and pulled her close, pressing the weapon to the side of her head.

Windham tensed. There wasn't much he could do without armor and weapons, but the sight of that terrified girl stabbed at his heart.

"Boys," said Wyatt, "I don't have time to figure out which one of these bastards betrayed us, so kill them all and let the devil sort them out." He inched toward the back of the stage, where a metal door led to who knew where.

There was a moment of confusion before the shooting started—a single moment when Windham had a chance to run for the portal and the safety of the *Asuka*. No one would have blamed him if he ran, not in the face of certain death. Typical armor could protect a soldier from two or three disruptor blasts, but the captain's civilian clothes offered no protection whatsoever. Any sane person would have fled, but not Windham. Call it madness or heroic idiocy, a Manthus never ran from danger—they confronted it head on and rushed in where angels feared to tread.

A nearby guard, the same one who had cleared Windham when he boarded the station, was raising his disruptor rifle in the second before the room erupted into chaos. The captain had just enough time to grab the man's wrist hard before the guard pulled the trigger. A superheated pulse of energy crackled across the room, catching an unarmed man square in the chest. He screamed as a burning hole appeared in the front of his shirt, but Windham felt no sympathy for a person who had come here to purchase a slave. As far as he was concerned, everyone in this room deserved to die.

Everyone, except the girl.

Windham had been trained as a Ranger of *Gilead*, an education that included multiple forms of hand fighting. The first lesson—the most important lesson—was to strike first and without mercy. He grapevined a foot around the guard's leg as they struggled with the disruptor rifle. Off balance,

the guard toppled forward to the metal floor and sprayed disruptor fire across the open room. He grunted when he hit the ground, just as Windham was expecting, and in that moment the captain seized the weapon and turned it on its owner.

"Please don't," begged the guard, but Windham had no mercy for this slaver. He pressed the top of the rifle to the man's chest and fired eight or ten blasts at point blank range. The guard's armor likely absorbed the first two, but not the others. He died screaming.

Windham dropped to the ground and used the dead guard's body as a shield. Propping himself up on his elbows, he opened fire into the crowded room, aiming at the red-armored reavers but not caring too much when one of his shots took out a buyer. Between the captain and the reavers, most of the civilians were slaughtered within a minute.

The captain pressed a button on his earpiece. "I need some rangers in here, STAT!"

The crossfire continued for another minute before reinforcements arrived. Dressed in black armor with the blue eagle of *Gilead* painted across their breastplates, the Rangers of *Gilead* were among the best warriors in known space. They entered the room through the gateway and secured the area almost immediately. Windham was back on his feet as soon as the reavers were dead, but there was no time to celebrate. It felt like an eternity since he had seen Captain Wyatt escape out the back with that poor girl, and he meant to rescue her. He turned to the nearest ranger.

"I need a pulse grenade."

"Sai?"

"Right now!"

"Yes, sai."

The ranger unclipped a pulse grenade from his utility belt and handed it to the captain. Windham took the weapon and made a B-line for the door at the back of the stage. It took the ranger a moment to realize that his commander was likely rushing headlong into danger before he followed behind.

Windham reached the door, pulled it open, and stared into a long corridor the stretched off into the distance. Wyatt and the girl were down there somewhere and he had to find them. He tapped his earpiece once again.

"Ward... Grayson, are you there?"

"I'm here."

"Keep a lock on the *Saladin*. Whatever you do, don't let them escape."

"I'm doing my best. All hell is—"

"Wyatt is trying to escape with a prisoner," Windham said, "we're not going to let that happen. "

"10-4." The transmission cut off abruptly, but Windham didn't have time to worry about that right now. He plunged into the corridor in search of his quarry.

Outside the station, *Gilead* was in the midst of a titanic space battle. Ward had dropped her cloak just as soon as they hacked into Chibok's gateway system, and the sight of a *Jerusalem*-class starship emerging out of the night must have given all of those little captains a

fright. *Gilead* was one of the largest and fastest ships ever built, and even though she was outnumbered, the odds were completely in her favor.

"Open a channel," said Ward.

"Yes, sai."

The first mate straightened in the captain's chair. "This is Grayson Ward, acting captain of the starship *Gilead*. Drop your shields, surrender your vessels, and prepare to be boarded."

Ward didn't expect anyone to comply, but some deep-seated sense of mercy prevented him from just slaughtering people without warning. On the other hand, these bastards had come out here to purchase human slaves, and he didn't expect them to turn themselves in without a fight. He wasn't surprised in the least when half a dozen small ships opened fire on *Gilead*.

"I warned you," he whispered to no one in particular.

Disruptor fire streamed across the darkness of space, but it crashed against *Gilead*'s shields and had no effect. The old ship was built for war, and her shield generators had been updated frequently over the centuries. Each disruptor blast revealed a section of the otherwise invisible shield for a fraction of a second, and then the energy was absorbed and another section lit up as enemy fire came in from all sides.

"Shields are holding," said the tactical officer.

"Target all ships and fire."

Disruptor cannons all over *Gilead* erupted with fire. Multiple blasts pulsed from the ship and toward the enemy fleet as timed windows opened and closed in the shields, allowing the destructive blasts to hit their targets.

Each blast reduced the enemy's shields, and once they collapsed, *Gilead* could destroy them with her torpedoes.

Not far away, on the far side of the station, the starship *Saladin* entered the fight. She was the only vessel here that gave Grayson pause. The *Saladin* was a legendary pirate ship, and her crew was notoriously cunning.

"The *Saladin* is powering up weapons," said the tactical officer.

Ward braced for impact. "Let's show those reavers what we're made of."

Windham found his quarry about a hundred meters down the escape corridor. Wyatt had paused in front of a gateway alcove, and was desperately trying to gain access to his ship with one hand while gripping the struggling slave girl with the other.

"Stop your cursed struggling, girl," Wyatt snapped. "I'll get this gateway unlocked in a minute and we'll—"

"Let her go, Braedon."

The reaver captain turned to face Windham. He was trembling with rage, you could see it on his face. How much money had he lost in this little excursion?

"Stop right there," said Wyatt. "Drop your weapon."

Windham slowed down momentarily, but instead of stopping, he tossed the pulse grenade he'd procured back in the auction room. It landed about halfway between the two warriors, and detonated upon impact. Everything went dark in a fifty-meter radius around the grenade. The grenade emitted an electromagnetic pulse that interfered with anything electronic, rendering it useless for about a minute. The corridor went dark, but there was still a bit of dim light from some glow-in-the-dark emergency panels built into the ceiling.

The reaver was momentarily stunned, and Windham took the opportunity to rush at his enemy. He barreled into the gloomy darkness, and when he drew near to Wyatt, he swung his now useless disruptor rifle at the reaver's face. Plastic met flesh with a sickening crack, and Wyatt stumbled backward several steps. But he did not fall.

The girl slithered out of her captor's grasp, and ran toward the perimeter of darkness created by the EMP.

Windham swung his disruptor again, but Wyatt caught it in mid-air and the two men struggled over the weapon. The reaver nearly gained control of the rifle, but Windham let go of it just as Wyatt tugged hard, and went toppling over backward. The disruptor went flying toward the girl.

The two captains hit the ground with a thud and wrestled in the darkness. Windham was on top at first, but his foe brought up an armored knee, hitting Manthus in the groin. He slumped over in agony as Wyatt climbed on top of him and wrapped his hands around Windham's throat. Time slowed as *Gilead's* captain struggled for breath.

Not far away, the girl darted back, grabbed the lost disruptor rifle, and stepped into the light. She stood on the perimeter of the EMP, raised the weapon, and fired nine blasts into the shadows. The first three were absorbed by Wyatt's armor, but the rest left half a dozen six-centimeter holes in the reaver's back. He slumped backward and thudded to the floor.

Windham caught his breath, then checked his enemy's vitals. He turned to face the terrified girl who was still clutching the disruptor rifle. "He's dead."

She stared at him, too traumatized to be ashamed at her nakedness. "Good."

Windham stood slowly, unbuttoning his shirt.

"What are you doing?" she demanded. She was still holding the disruptor and clearly knew how to use it.

"Put this on," said the captain. He handed her the shirt and then turned his back so that she could cover herself in private.

The lights came back on while they were walking back to the auction room.

"What's your name?" Windham asked as they walked.

"Eowyn Morrison."

"Your father is the governor of Avalon."

"Yeah." Her head slumped, as if the weight of everything that had happened had fallen suddenly upon her brow, "I'm Captain Windham Manthus of the starship *Gilead.*"

"*Gilead?*" She looked up, surprised.

"That's right. Your father asked me to help... to come here and rescue the children of Avalon. But it looks like you had the situation under control yourself."

She gave out a bitter laugh.

"You were very brave, Eowyn. How old are you?"

"Eighteen."

"You have the spirit of a warrior."

"I don't want to be a warrior," she said. "I just want to live in peace."

"As do we all," said the captain. "As do we all."

THE *SALADIN* HIT *GILEAD* WITH A MASsive burst of disruptor fire and the old ship's shields nearly buckled.

"We're down to fifteen percent," said the tactical officer.

"Direct all our disruptors at the *Saladin* and fire," ordered Grayson.

"Yes, sai."

Gilead floated in a graveyard of destroyed enemy vessels. The smart ones had fled, realizing that was their only hope for survival. The remaining enemy ships had put up quite a struggle, but most were no match for *Gilead* and were easily destroyed. Only a handful remained. The *Saladin* was the cream of the crop, and she was fighting for her life. These space pirates had been plaguing *Gilead*'s barony for decades, and now Grayson had an opportunity to end their conflict once and for all.

Half a hundred bursts of disrupter fire tore across the black and crackled against *Saladin*'s shields; they buckled.

The commander of the *Saladin* had a second—maybe two—to decide if they would stay and die or live to fight another day. He chose to retreat. The pirate vessel vanished as it went to warp, leaving her captain dying on the floor of Chibok Station.

"Good work," Grayson said. "Now, let's bring our people home."

THE CHILDREN OF AVALON BOARDED *Gilead*, thankful that their ordeal had not ended in a life of slavery. As the old ship left orbit, Windham ordered a spread of torpedoes launched against Chibok Station, utterly destroying that particular den of thieves. *Gilead* proceeded back to Cheron-4 at maximum warp, and as the hours stretched past, he became acquainted with the people he had helped rescue. These young people—there were children among the refuges, but many were in their late teens or early twenties—were the future of Avalon, and he wanted them to see *Gilead* as a friend when their own turns came to lead their community. As for Eowyn Morrison, she seemed particularly aloof. She had been exposed to a room full of monsters who wanted to commit her to a life of slavery, and even though she had escaped that terrible fate, she carried the weight of that alternate future on her young shoulders. The governor threw an enormous celebration when *Gilead* reached Cheron-4. Everyone in Avalon attended the party, and speeches were made as thankful parents vowed their loyalty to Windham and his descendents. During the celebration, Governor Morrison formally restored Avalon's relationship with the starship *Gilead* to the cheers of the gathered assembly. As the citizens of Avalon and the crew of *Gilead* watched, Morrison led his daughter onto the makeshift stage at the center of the celebration. He motioned for the crowd to hush, and they obeyed him, sensing that something significant was about to happen.

"Thank you, Captain Manthus, for returning my daughter to me."

"It was an honor," Windham said.

Eowyn looked painfully shy standing there in front of everyone. She tried to maintain eye contact with Windham, but every time he looked at her all he could see was fear in her eyes.

"I'm not sure how to say this, sai, so I'll just come out with it." The governor looked nervous, like whatever he was about to say was weighing heavily on his heart. "It is customary to seal an agreement with a marriage. My daughter was promised to the prince of the starship *Jericho*, but of course I cannot in good conscience honor that agreement."

"Of course not." Windham's blood stirred at the thought of beautiful Eowyn in the arms of Captain Gaines's idiot son. She seemed so troubled on their voyage home, and he wanted so much to see joy and hope in her eyes.

"I would be honored," Morrison said, "if you would take her as your wife."

This sort of thing had always bothered Windham—men of power arranging their daughter's marriages without their consent—but after the collapse of the Union, such things had become customary in the outer baronies. He could imagine another life for himself—one where he wasn't responsible for a starship and an entire barony. What would it be like to live on farm outside of Avalon, tending livestock and falling in love with a country girl as they worked the land together? Unfortunately, this was not the life that fate had given him, and Windham knew that it would be a terrible insult if he were to refuse the governor's offer.

"I would be honored to marry your daughter," said the captain.

"Then let it be so," the governor said. He took Eowyn's hands and joined them with Windham's. They stood there, before the multitude, and looked into each other's eyes under a canopy of stars.

"I know you've endured a terrible trauma," Windham whispered. "And I know that this must be difficult for you, but I will do my best to be a good husband to you. And I hope that you can come to care for me."

Eowyn smiled, the fear in her eyes momentarily replaced but a look of hope. "I'll try," she said, "if you could just give me some time."

"We have all the time in the world," Windham said. But, unfortunately, they did not.

There were tears in her eyes, but there was a hint of a smile on her lips. She reached out and touched his bare face. "I liked you better with the beard."

Windham grinned. "I'll grow one for you."

"I'm frightened. A week ago I was tending my garden and dreading my impending wedding to a man I've only met once. And now... everything has happened so fast."

"For me, too," said the captain. "But we don't have to get married tomorrow. We can get to know each other first."

"I'd like that." Eowyn lowered her eyes, clearly embarrassed by whatever she was about to say next. "You... you're supposed to kiss me now, I think, to seal the arrangement. I've never..."

She blushed pink.

Windham took her by the shoulders, leaning in close, and kissed her gently on the lips. The gathered crowd cheered as the most powerful man in this region of space embraced one of their own.

Outside of town, up on a hill that overlooked Avalon, was a cemetery where the bodies of those slain in the reaver attack were laid to rest. A white marble pillar served as a memorial to the fallen, and atop this pillar, mounted on a spike, was the severed head of Braedon Wyatt. His rein of terror was over, but the *Saladin* was still out there, along with a host of other troubles. Space was a dark and frightening place, but there was one shining beacon of hope and justice in the black—the starship *Gilead*, Warden of the Night.

THE END

WINDHAM'S ADVENTURES CONTINUE IN

STARSHIP GILEAD

RELICS OF UTOPIA

AVAILABLE WHEREVER BOOKS ARE SOLD

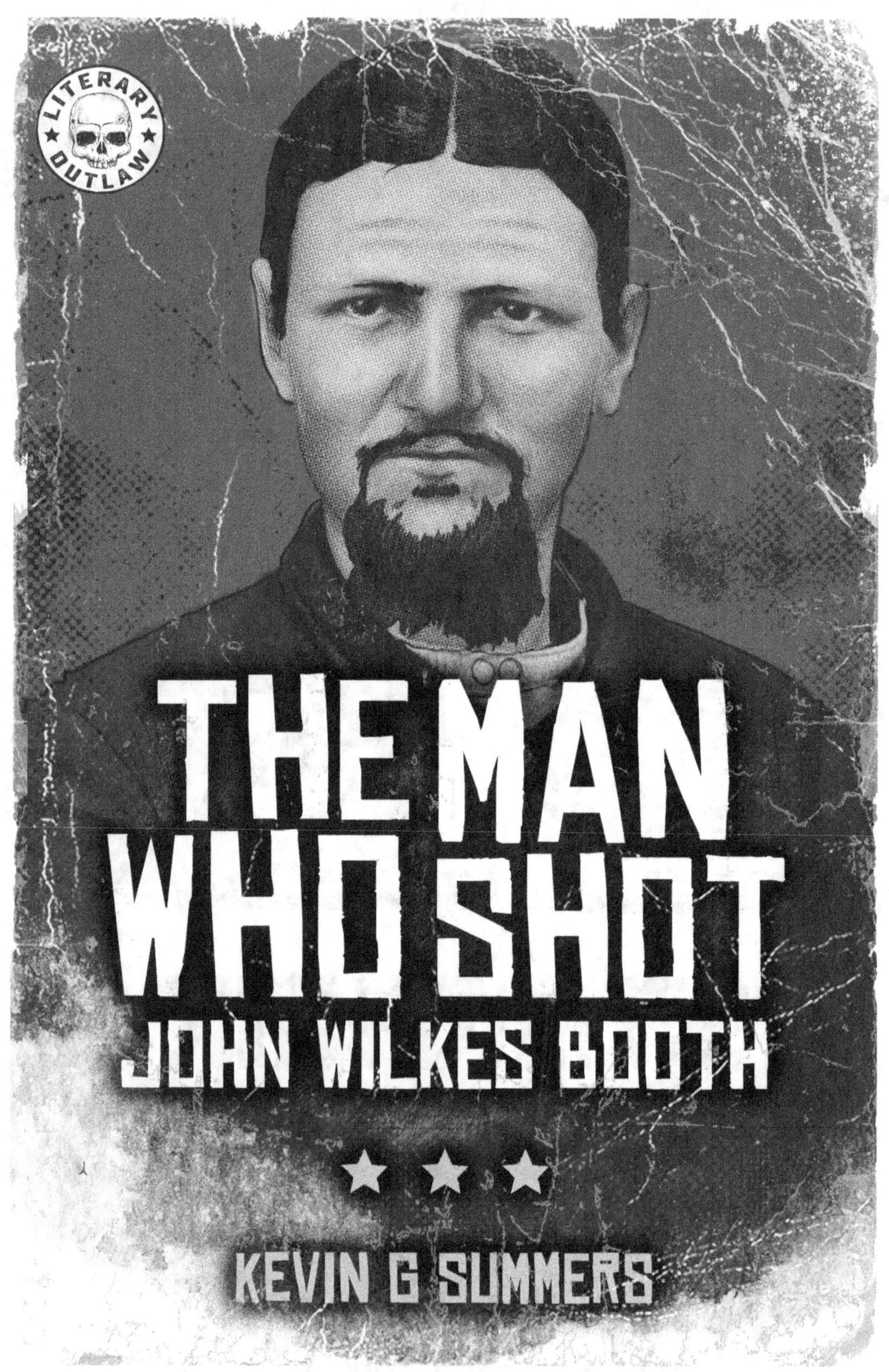

THE FOLLOWING STORY IS A PREQUEL TO THE NOVEL
LITERARY OUTLAW
THE MAN WHO SHOT
JOHN WILKES BOOTH
KEVIN G SUMMERS
AVAILABLE WHEREVER BOOKS ARE SOLD

THE
Paradise Ledger
PRESENTS
The PARABLE of The SOWER

By Kevin G. Summers And James Hale

WE LIVED ON MY FATHERS OLD PLANTATION JUST EAST OF HERE. EIGHTEEN-HUNDRED ACRES OF SUGARCANE RIGHT ON THE MISSISSIPPI. IT WAS SIMPLY BREATHTAKING.
IT WAS THE HAPPIEST TIME IN MY LIFE. MY HUSBAND, EDWARD, AND ME, AND OUR THREE BOYS — WE HAD EVERYTHING A FAMILY COULD DESIRE UNTIL THAT... THAT NIGGER LOVER STARTED HIS WAR.
OUR OLDEST, ROBERT, DIED FIGHTING THE YANKEES. THEN WE WERE TOLD WE HAD TO FREE OUR SLAVES... I THOUGHT WE WERE RUINED.

BUT EDWARD HAD A PLAN. HE HEARD ABOUT THESE WORKERS THEY HAVE DOWN IN HAITI, SO HE HIRED THIS VOODOO WOMAN FROM NAWLINS TO DELIVER US A NEW CROP OF SLAVES.
BUT THESE SLAVES...
...I DON'T KNOW HOW, BUT THAT WITCH USED HER VOODOO MAGIC TO RAISE UP THE DEAD.

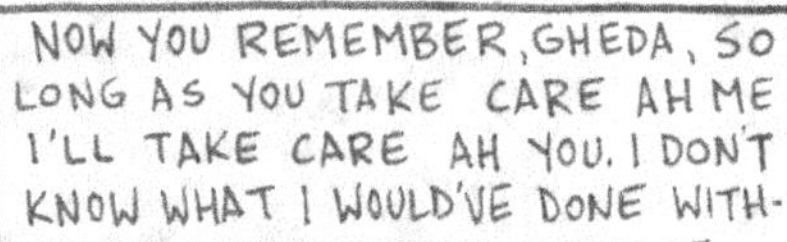

SUDDENLY WE HAD MONEY AGAIN. I WAS SO HAPPY I TOOK A TRIP TO BATON ROUGE TO VISIT MY SISTER. THAT WAS IN THE SUMMER OF '68.

NOW YOU REMEMBER, GHEDA, SO LONG AS YOU TAKE CARE AH ME I'LL TAKE CARE AH YOU. I DON'T KNOW WHAT I WOULD'VE DONE WITHOUT THOSE...
...WORKERS YOU CONJURED UP FOR ME.

GOODNIGHT, GHEDA. MAKE SURE BREAKFAST IS ON THE TABLE WHEN I GET UP.

THE NEXT MORNING...
TI BON ANGE.
TI BON ANGE
TOUYE...
...OU METRIZE.

YOUR MOTHER SENDS HER LOVE AND WANTS ME TO REMIND YOU...
krrrreeeaaak
WHAT WAS THAT?
PROBABLY JUST MY IMAGINATION...

KA
KA
KRAAK
KRAAK
AAAAHHHH!

RETURN TO YOUR ENDLESS SLEEP.
YOU HAVE EARNED YOUR REST, MY BROTHERS.
SHE WAS WAITING FOR ME WHEN I RETURNED HOME.

GHEDA TOLD ME EVERTHING SHE HAD DONE... THAT EDWARD HAD DONE.
WHY DID SHE LET YOU LIVE?
TO PUNISH ME. TO REMIND ME OF THAT OLD PROVERB...
FOR WHATSOEVER A MAN SOWETH, THAT SHALL HE ALSO REAP.
THE END

2 B R 0 2 B
BY KURT VONNEGUT, JR.

Everything was perfectly swell.

There were no prisons, no slums, no insane asylums, no cripples, no poverty, no wars.

All diseases were conquered. So was old age.

Death, barring accidents, was an adventure for volunteers.

The population of the United States was stabilized at forty-million souls.

One bright morning in the Chicago Lying-in Hospital, a man named Edward K. Wehling, Jr., waited for his wife to give birth. He was the only man waiting. Not many people were born a day any more.

Wehling was fifty-six, a mere stripling in a population whose average age was one hundred and twenty-nine.

X-rays had revealed that his wife was going to have triplets. The children would be his first.

Young Wehling was hunched in his chair, his head in his hand. He was so rumpled, so still and colorless as to be virtually invisible. His camouflage was perfect, since the waiting room had a disorderly and demoralized air, too. Chairs and ashtrays had been moved away from the walls. The floor was paved with spattered dropcloths.

The room was being redecorated. It was being redecorated as a memorial to a man who had volunteered to die.

A sardonic old man, about two hundred years old, sat on a stepladder, painting a mural he did not like. Back in the days when people aged visibly, his age would have been guessed at thirty-five or so. Aging had touched him that much before the cure for aging was found.

The mural he was working on depicted a very neat garden. Men and women in white, doctors and nurses, turned the soil, planted seedlings, sprayed bugs, spread fertilizer.

Men and women in purple uniforms pulled up weeds, cut down plants that were old and sickly, raked leaves, carried refuse to trash-burners.

Never, never, never—not even in medieval Holland nor old Japan—had a garden been more formal, been better tended. Every plant had all the loam, light, water, air and nourishment it could use.

A hospital orderly came down the corridor, singing under his breath a popular song:

If you don't like my kisses, honey,
Here's what I will do:
I'll go see a girl in purple,
Kiss this sad world toodle-oo.
If you don't want my lovin',
Why should I take up all this space?
I'll get off this old planet,
Let some sweet baby have my place.

The orderly looked in at the mural and the muralist. "Looks so real," he said, "I can practically imagine I'm standing in the middle of it."

"What makes you think you're not in it?" said the painter. He gave a satiric smile. "It's called 'The Happy Garden of Life,' you know."

"That's good of Dr. Hitz," said the orderly.

*

HE WAS REFERRING TO ONE OF THE male figures in white, whose head was a portrait of Dr. Benjamin Hitz, the hospital's Chief Obstetrician. Hitz was a blindingly handsome man.

"Lot of faces still to fill in," said the orderly. He meant that the faces of many of the figures in the mural were still blank. All blanks were to be filled with portraits of important people on either the hospital staff or from the Chicago Office of the Federal Bureau of Termination.

"Must be nice to be able to make pictures that look like something," said the orderly.

The painter's face curdled with scorn. "You think I'm proud of this daub?" he said. "You think this is my idea of what life really looks like?"

"What's your idea of what life looks like?" said the orderly.

The painter gestured at a foul dropcloth. "There's a good picture of it," he said. "Frame that, and you'll have a picture a damn sight more honest than this one."

"You're a gloomy old duck, aren't you?" said the orderly.

"Is that a crime?" said the painter.

The orderly shrugged. "If you don't like it here, Grandpa—" he said, and he finished the thought with the trick telephone number that people who didn't want to live any more were supposed to call. The zero in the telephone number he pronounced "naught."

The number was: "2 B R 0 2 B."

It was the telephone number of an institution whose fanciful sobriquets included: "Automat," "Birdland," "Cannery," "Catbox," "De-louser," "Easy-go," "Good-by, Mother," "Happy Hooligan," "Kiss-me-quick," "Lucky Pierre," "Sheepdip," "Waring Blendor," "Weep-no-more" and "Why Worry?"

"To be or not to be" was the telephone number of the municipal gas chambers of the Federal Bureau of Termination.

*

THE PAINTER THUMBED HIS NOSE AT the orderly. "When I decide it's time to go," he said, "it won't be at the Sheepdip."

"A do-it-yourselfer, eh?" said the orderly. "Messy business, Grandpa. Why don't you have a little consideration for the people who have to clean up after you?"

The painter expressed with an obscenity his lack of concern for the tribulations of his survivors. "The world could do with a good deal more mess, if you ask me," he said.

The orderly laughed and moved on.

Wehling, the waiting father, mumbled something without raising his head. And then he fell silent again.

A coarse, formidable woman strode into the waiting room on spike heels. Her shoes, stockings, trench coat, bag and overseas cap were all purple, the purple the painter called "the color of grapes on Judgment Day."

The medallion on her purple musette bag was the seal of the Service Division of the Federal Bureau of Termination, an eagle perched on a turnstile.

The woman had a lot of facial hair—an unmistakable mustache, in fact. A curious thing about gas-chamber hostesses was that, no matter how lovely and feminine they were when recruited, they all sprouted mustaches within five years or so.

"Is this where I'm supposed to come?" she said to the painter.

"A lot would depend on what your business was," he said. "You aren't about to have a baby, are you?"

"They told me I was supposed to pose for some picture," she said. "My name's Leora Duncan." She waited.

"And you dunk people," he said.

"What?" she said.

"Skip it," he said.

"That sure is a beautiful picture," she said. "Looks just like heaven or something."

"Or something," said the painter. He took a list of names from his smock pocket. "Duncan, Duncan, Duncan," he said, scanning the list. "Yes—here

you are. You're entitled to be immortalized. See any faceless body here you'd like me to stick your head on? We've got a few choice ones left."

She studied the mural bleakly. "Gee," she said, "they're all the same to me. I don't know anything about art."

"A body's a body, eh?" he said. "All righty. As a master of fine art, I recommend this body here." He indicated a faceless figure of a woman who was carrying dried stalks to a trash-burner.

"Well," said Leora Duncan, "that's more the disposal people, isn't it? I mean, I'm in service. I don't do any disposing."

The painter clapped his hands in mock delight. "You say you don't know anything about art, and then you prove in the next breath that you know more about it than I do! Of course the sheave-carrier is wrong for a hostess! A snipper, a pruner—that's more your line." He pointed to a figure in purple who was sawing a dead branch from an apple tree. "How about her?" he said. "You like her at all?"

"Gosh—" she said, and she blushed and became humble—"that—that puts me right next to Dr. Hitz."

"That upsets you?" he said.

"Good gravy, no!" she said. "It's—it's just such an honor."

"Ah, You... you admire him, eh?" he said.

"Who doesn't admire him?" she said, worshiping the portrait of Hitz. It was the portrait of a tanned, white-haired, omnipotent Zeus, two hundred and forty years old. "Who doesn't admire him?" she said again.

"He was responsible for setting up the very first gas chamber in Chicago."

"Nothing would please me more," said the painter, "than to put you next to him for all time. Sawing off a limb—that strikes you as appropriate?"

"That is kind of like what I do," she said. She was demure about what she did. What she did was make people comfortable while she killed them.

*

AND, WHILE LEORA DUNCAN WAS POS-ing for her portrait, into the waiting-room bounded Dr. Hitz himself. He was seven feet tall, and he boomed with importance, accomplishments, and the joy of living.

"Well, Miss Duncan! Miss Duncan!" he said, and he made a joke. "What are you doing here?" he said. "This isn't where the people leave. This is where they come in!"

"We're going to be in the same picture together," she said shyly.

"Good!" said Dr. Hitz heartily. "And, say, isn't that some picture?"

"I sure am honored to be in it with you," she said.

"Let me tell you," he said, "I'm honored to be in it with you. Without women like you, this wonderful world we've got wouldn't be possible."

He saluted her and moved toward the door that led to the delivery rooms. "Guess what was just born," he said.

"I can't," she said.

"Triplets!" he said.

"Triplets!" she said. She was exclaiming over the legal implications of triplets.

The law said that no newborn child could survive unless the parents of the child could find someone who would volunteer to die. Triplets, if they were all to live, called for three volunteers.

"Do the parents have three volunteers?" said Leora Duncan.

"Last I heard," said Dr. Hitz, "they had one, and were trying to scrape another two up."

"I don't think they made it," she said. "Nobody made three appointments with us. Nothing but singles going through today, unless somebody called in after I left. What's the name?"

"Wehling," said the waiting father, sitting up, red-eyed and frowzy. "Edward K. Wehling, Jr., is the name of the happy father-to-be."

He raised his right hand, looked at a spot on the wall, gave a hoarsely wretched chuckle. "Present," he said.

"Oh, Mr. Wehling," said Dr. Hitz, "I didn't see you."

"The invisible man," said Wehling.

"They just phoned me that your triplets have been born," said Dr. Hitz. "They're all fine, and so is the mother. I'm on my way in to see them now."

"Hooray," said Wehling emptily.

"You don't sound very happy," said Dr. Hitz.

"What man in my shoes wouldn't be happy?" said Wehling. He gestured with his hands to symbolize care-free simplicity. "All I have to do is pick out which one of the triplets is going to live, then deliver my maternal grandfather to the Happy Hooligan, and come back here with a receipt."

*

DR. HITZ BECAME RATHER SEVERE with Wehling, towered over him. "You don't believe in population control, Mr. Wehling?" he said.

"I think it's perfectly keen," said Wehling tautly.

"Would you like to go back to the good old days, when the population of the Earth was twenty billion—about to become forty billion, then eighty billion, then one hundred and sixty billion? Do you know what a drupelet is, Mr. Wehling?" said Hitz.

"Nope," said Wehling sulkily.

"A drupelet, Mr. Wehling, is one of the little knobs, one of the little pulpy grains of a blackberry," said Dr. Hitz. "Without population control, human beings would now be packed on this surface of this old planet like drupelets on a blackberry! Think of it!"

Wehling continued to stare at the same spot on the wall.

"In the year 2000," said Dr. Hitz, "before scientists stepped in and laid down the law, there wasn't even enough drinking water to go around, and nothing to eat but sea-weed—and still people insisted on their right to reproduce like jackrabbits. And their right, if possible, to live forever."

"I want those kids," said Wehling quietly. "I want all three of them."

"Of course you do," said Dr. Hitz. "That's only human."

"I don't want my grandfather to die, either," said Wehling.

"Nobody's really happy about taking a close relative to the Catbox," said Dr. Hitz gently, sympathetically.

"I wish people wouldn't call it that," said Leora Duncan.

"What?" said Dr. Hitz.

"I wish people wouldn't call it 'the Catbox,' and things like that," she said. "It gives people the wrong impression."

"You're absolutely right," said Dr. Hitz. "Forgive me." He corrected himself, gave the municipal gas chambers their official title, a title no one ever used in conversation. "I should have said, 'Ethical Suicide Studios,'" he said.

"That sounds so much better," said Leora Duncan.

"This child of yours—whichever one you decide to keep, Mr. Wehling," said Dr. Hitz. "He or she is going to live on a happy, roomy, clean, rich planet, thanks to population control. In a garden like that mural there." He shook his head. "Two centuries ago, when I was a young man, it was a hell that nobody thought could last another twenty years. Now centuries of peace and plenty stretch before us as far as the imagination cares to travel."

He smiled luminously.

The smile faded as he saw that Wehling had just drawn a revolver.

Wehling shot Dr. Hitz dead. "There's room for one—a great big one," he said.

And then he shot Leora Duncan. "It's only death," he said to her as she fell. "There! Room for two."

And then he shot himself, making room for all three of his children.

Nobody came running. Nobody, seemingly, heard the shots.

The painter sat on the top of his stepladder, looking down reflectively on the sorry scene.

*

THE PAINTER PONDERED THE MOURN-ful puzzle of life demanding to be born and, once born, demanding to be fruitful ... to multiply and to live as long as possible—to do all that on a very small planet that would have to last forever.

All the answers that the painter could think of were grim. Even grimmer, surely, than a Catbox, a Happy Hooligan, an Easy Go. He thought of war. He thought of plague. He thought of starvation.

He knew that he would never paint again. He let his paintbrush fall to the drop-cloths below. And then he decided he had had about enough of life in the Happy Garden of Life, too, and he came slowly down from the ladder.

He took Wehling's pistol, really intending to shoot himself.

But he didn't have the nerve.

And then he saw the telephone booth in the corner of the room. He went to it, dialed the well-remembered number: "2 B R 0 2 B."

"Federal Bureau of Termination," said the very warm voice of a hostess.

"How soon could I get an appointment?" he asked, speaking very carefully.

"We could probably fit you in late this afternoon, sir," she said. "It might even be earlier, if we get a cancellation."

"All right," said the painter, "fit me in, if you please." And he gave her his name, spelling it out.

"Thank you, sir," said the hostess. "Your city thanks you; your country thanks you; your planet thanks you. But the deepest thanks of all is from future generations."

THE END

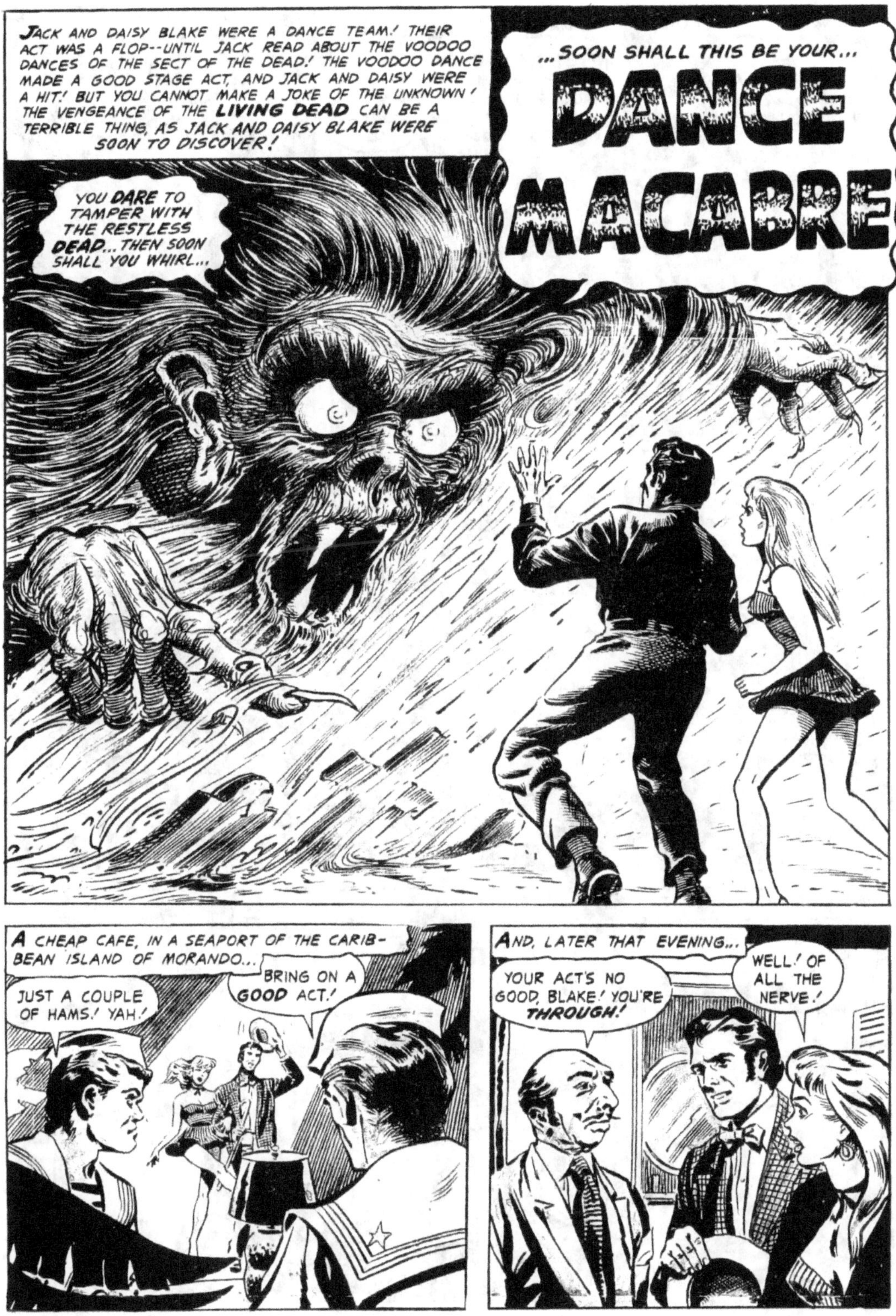

Jack and Daisy Blake were a dance team! Their act was a flop--until Jack read about the voodoo dances of the sect of the dead! The voodoo dance made a good stage act, and Jack and Daisy were a hit! But you cannot make a joke of the unknown! The vengeance of the **living dead** can be a terrible thing, as Jack and Daisy Blake were soon to discover!

...SOON SHALL THIS BE YOUR...

DANCE MACABRE

You **dare** to tamper with the restless **dead**...then soon shall you whirl...

THAT NIGHT, IN THEIR HOTEL ROOM...
WE'VE GOT TO CHANGE THE ACT, OR WE'RE SUNK! EVEN IN A DUMP LIKE THIS WE DON'T GET BY! GOT TO GET SOME-THING NOVEL
YEAH? LIKE WHAT?

THEN JACK HAD A BRIGHT IDEA!
THESE SUPERSTITIOUS NATIVES ARE ALWAYS TALKING ABOUT VOODOO-ISM! MUST BE SOME WEIRD VOODOO DANCES, HUH?
SEARCH ME?

NEXT DAY...
WHAT'S THIS VOO-DOO CULT, DU MORT, I HEAR TALK ABOUT?
THE DEAD ONES! DO NOT PRY IN-TO IT, M'SIEU! SUCH THINGS ARE NOT FOR THE LIVING!

THE NATIVES WERE AFRAID TO TALK OF IT! BUT IN THE LIBRARY...
HERE IT IS! CULT OF THE RESTLESS DEAD! HAH! DEAD PEOPLE WHO CAN'T STAY IN THEIR GRAVES! SOUNDS SWELL!

"AND IT IS SAID THAT PEOPLE WHO HAVE DIED BY VIOLENCE OFTEN STALK BY NIGHT IN UNHOLY RITUALS OF THE LIVING DEAD! MANY INSTANCES ARE ON RECORD WHERE THEY HAVE BEEN SEEN DANCING!"

HE TOLD DAISY ABOUT IT...
NOVEL, EH? SWELL STUFF FOR US, KID!
UGH! IT SURE SOUNDS WEIRD!

WEIRD? SURE! BUT, LISTEN--HERE'S THE TOPPER! WE'LL BURLESQUE IT! GRUESOME STUFF! IT'LL LAND US ON BROADWAY IN A YEAR!
WELL, IF YOU THINK WE CAN PUT IT OVER, JACK...

THEY WORKED HARD ON IT! THE MANAGER OF THE LITTLE CAFE GAVE THEM ANOTHER TRY, AND...
WOW!
IT'S SURE GRUESOME!
WHAT CREEPY STUFF!

HA-HA! THAT'S FUNNY!
THEY'RE GOOD!

THE NOVEL ACT WAS A BIG HIT! THE FAME OF JACK AND DAISY BLAKE SPREAD THROUGHOUT THE ISLAND! BUT ONE NIGHT...
INFIDELS! PROFANERS OF THE DEAD! YOU SHALL BE PUNISHED!
WHA--?

THE FATE THAT WAS OURS SHALL BE YOURS! DEATH BY VIOLENCE! THE TIME WILL COME--YOU CANNOT ESCAPE IT! YOU WILL MAKE MONEY, YES! BUT IT WILL CAUSE YOU BOTH TO BE MURDERED!
OHHHH!

A FRIGHTENING THING! BUT THEY TRIED TO LAUGH IT OFF, AND...
I--I GUESS I'M SCARED, DOING THIS!
NONSENSE! HOW CAN THE DEAD HURT US? WE ONLY IMAGINED THAT WE SAW THEM, ANYWAY! WE'RE GONNA GET RICH KID!

THE MONEY CAME IN! SOON THEY WERE APPEARING IN CAPITAL CITIES IN THE BIG MUNICIPAL THEATRE.!
BRAVO! WONDERFUL!
REAL ART!

BUT ALWAYS IT SEEMED THAT THE RESTLESS, ENRAGED SPIRITS OF THE DEAD WERE WATCHING THEM...
THERE THEY ARE! WATCHING US! ALWAYS WATCHING US!

AND SOMETIMES AT NIGHT..
SOON! YOU WILL BOTH BE MURDERED! BEWARE.!
GET AWAY FROM US! LEAVE US ALONE!

THEIR TERROR GREW! WOULD SOMEBODY TRY TO KILL THEM? NOW THEY WERE SUSPICIOUS OF EVERYONE THEY MET.!
WELL, HELLO THERE! CONGRATULATIONS! YOU SURE HIT THE BIG TIME.!
WHAT A QUEER LOOK HE'S GOT! WOULD HE DARE--
THANKS, TOM! YEAH, WE'RE DOING ALL RIGHT.!

THEY LIVED LIVES OF TORTURE! ALL THEIR FOOD AND DRINK TASTED QUEER! SHADOWS ALWAYS SEEM TO BE HOLDING AN ASSASSIN.!
JACK, WE'VE GOT TO GET ANOTHER ACT.!
GIVE UP BIG MONEY? DON'T BE A FOOL!

YOU'RE THE FOOL! DO YOU WANT TO GET US MURDERED?
HAH! THAT STUFF'S ONLY FOR IGNORANT NATIVES.!

THEIR TAUT NERVES WERE FRAYED BY TERROR! THEY OFTEN QUARRELED...
DON'T YOU TELL ME WHAT WE'RE GOING TO DO! I'M THE BRAINS OF THIS OUTFIT!
YEAH? WHO PUTS THE ACT OVER? NOT YOU!

THEIR MUTUAL TERROR BROUGHT HATRED!
SHE'LL DOUBLECROSS ME IF SHE GETS A CHANCE!...
HE'LL GET US MURDERED! I DON'T WANT TO DIE, JUST BECAUSE OF HIS GREED!

AND SOON AFTER THAT...
HELLO, TESSIE!
HI!

SURE WISH I COULD MAKE A HIT LIKE YOU AND DAISY! THERE'S MY CUE! 'BYE NOW!
...IF DAISY WANTS TO QUIT ME-- OKAY! TESSIE'D BE A BETTER PARTNER, ANYWAY!...

SHE'S ASLEEP! YOU CAN DO IT!
SURE I CAN!...

AND THAT SAME NIGHT...
AW, SHUT UP! GO AHEAD AND QUIT ME! I'D BE GLAD TO GET RID OF YOU!
ALL RIGHT, I WILL, IF YOU'LL GIVE ME MY SHARE OF OUR MONEY!

AND LATER, WHEN DAISY WAS ASLEEP...
WHAT ARE YOU AFRAID OF? YOU CAN DO IT!
WHY NOT? THAT WOULD FIX EVERYTHING!...

WHA--? ULP!
HA-HA!
HURRY, DAISY! YOU PLANNED IT, DIDN'T YOU? YOU HID THAT KNIFE UNDER YOUR PILLOW! QUICK! STAB HIM! THEN YOU'LL HAVE ALL THE MONEY!
UGH!
THE MURDEROUS JACK BLAKE COULD FEEL HIS SENSES FADING! BUT STILL HE HAD THE STRENGH TO CLING WITH HIS DEATH GRIP --UNTIL, AT LAST...
HA-HA-HA! BOTH OF THEM--DEAD!
DOOMED TO BE MUR-DERED--AND SO THEY KILLED EACH OTHER! HA-HA-HA!
THE RESTLESS DEAD! STRANGE THINGS HAPPEN ON THE LITTLE TROPIC ISLAND OF MORANDO! THEY SAY THAT NOW, OFTEN AT NIGHT...
...FOR ETERNITY!

THE REPAIRER OF REPUTATIONS

BY ROBERT W. CHAMBERS

1

«Ne raillons pas les fous; leur folie dure plus longtemps que la nôtre.... Voila toute la différence. »

TOWARD THE END OF THE YEAR 1920 the Government of the United States had practically completed the programme, adopted during the last months of President Winthrop's administration. The country was apparently tranquil. Everybody knows how the Tariff and Labour questions were settled. The war with Germany, incident on that country's seizure of the Samoan Islands, had left no visible scars upon the republic, and the temporary occupation of Norfolk by the invading army had been forgotten in the joy over repeated naval victories, and the subsequent ridiculous plight of General Von Gartenlaube's forces in the State of New Jersey. The Cuban and Hawaiian investments had paid one hundred per cent and the territory of Samoa was well worth its cost as a coaling station. The country was in a superb state of defence. Every coast city had been well supplied with land fortifications; the army under the parental eye of the General Staff, organized according to the Prussian system, had been increased to 300,000 men, with a territorial reserve of a million; and six magnificent squadrons of cruisers and battle-ships patrolled the six stations of the navigable seas, leaving a steam reserve amply fitted to control home waters. The gentlemen from the West had at last been constrained to acknowledge that a college for the training of diplomats was as necessary as law schools are for the training of barristers; consequently we were no longer represented abroad by incompetent patriots. The nation was prosperous; Chicago, for a moment paralyzed after a second great fire, had risen from its ruins, white and imperial, and more beautiful than the white city which had been built for its plaything in 1893. Everywhere good architecture was replacing bad, and even in New York, a sudden craving for decency had swept away a great portion of the existing horrors. Streets had been widened, properly paved and lighted, trees had been planted, squares laid out, elevated structures demolished and underground roads built to replace them. The new government buildings and barracks were fine bits of architecture, and the long system of stone quays which completely surrounded the island had been turned into parks which proved a god-send to the population. The subsidizing of the state theatre and state opera brought its own reward. The United States National Academy of Design was much like European institutions of the same kind. Nobody envied the Secretary of Fine Arts, either his cabinet position or his portfolio. The Secretary of Forestry and Game Preservation had a much easier time, thanks to the new system of National Mounted Police. We had profited well by the latest treaties with France and England; the exclusion of foreign-born Jews as a measure of self-preservation, the settlement of the new independent negro state of Suanee, the checking of immigration, the new laws concerning naturalization, and the gradual centralization of power in the executive all contributed to national calm and prosperity. When the Government solved the Indian problem and squadrons of Indian cavalry scouts in native costume were substituted for the pitiable organizations tacked on to the tail of skeletonized regiments by a former Secretary of War, the nation drew a long sigh of relief. When, after the colossal Congress of Religions, bigotry and intolerance were laid in their graves and kindness and charity began to draw warring sects together, many thought the millennium had arrived, at least in the new world which after all is a world by itself.

But self-preservation is the first law, and the United States had to look on in helpless sorrow as Germany, Italy, Spain and Belgium writhed in the throes of Anarchy, while Russia,

watching from the Caucasus, stooped and bound them one by one.

In the city of New York the summer of 1899 was signalized by the dismantling of the Elevated Railroads. The summer of 1900 will live in the memories of New York people for many a cycle; the Dodge Statue was removed in that year. In the following winter began that agitation for the repeal of the laws prohibiting suicide which bore its final fruit in the month of April, 1920, when the first Government Lethal Chamber was opened on Washington Square.

I had walked down that day from Dr. Archer's house on Madison Avenue, where I had been as a mere formality. Ever since that fall from my horse, four years before, I had been troubled at times with pains in the back of my head and neck, but now for months they had been absent, and the doctor sent me away that day saying there was nothing more to be cured in me. It was hardly worth his fee to be told that; I knew it myself. Still I did not grudge him the money. What I minded was the mistake which he made at first. When they picked me up from the pavement where I lay unconscious, and somebody had mercifully sent a bullet through my horse's head, I was carried to Dr. Archer, and he, pronouncing my brain affected, placed me in his private asylum where I was obliged to endure treatment for insanity. At last he decided that I was well, and I, knowing that my mind had always been as sound as his, if not sounder, "paid my tuition" as he jokingly called it, and left. I told him, smiling, that I would get even with him for his mistake, and he laughed heartily, and asked me to call once in a while. I did so, hoping for a chance to even up accounts, but he gave me none, and I told him I would wait.

The fall from my horse had fortunately left no evil results; on the contrary it had changed my whole character for the better. From a lazy young man about town, I had become active, energetic, temperate, and above all—oh, above all else—ambitious. There was only one thing which troubled me, I laughed at my own uneasiness, and yet it troubled me.

During my convalescence I had bought and read for the first time, *The King in Yellow*. I remember after finishing the first act that it occurred to me that I had better stop. I started up and flung the book into the fireplace; the volume struck the barred grate and fell open on the hearth in the firelight. If I had not caught a glimpse of the opening words in the second act I should never have finished it, but as I stooped to pick it up, my eyes became riveted to the open page, and with a cry of terror, or perhaps it was of joy so poignant that I suffered in every nerve, I snatched the thing out of the coals and crept shaking to my bedroom, where I read it and reread it, and wept and laughed and trembled with a horror which at times assails me yet. This is the thing that troubles me, for I cannot forget Carcosa where black stars hang in the heavens; where the shadows of men's thoughts lengthen in the afternoon, when the twin suns sink into the lake of Hali; and my mind will bear for ever the memory of the Pallid Mask. I pray

God will curse the writer, as the writer has cursed the world with this beautiful, stupendous creation, terrible in its simplicity, irresistible in its truth—a world which now trembles before the King in Yellow. When the French Government seized the translated copies which had just arrived in Paris, London, of course, became eager to read it. It is well known how the book spread like an infectious disease, from city to city, from continent to continent, barred out here, confiscated there, denounced by Press and pulpit, censured even by the most advanced of literary anarchists. No definite principles had been violated in those wicked pages, no doctrine promulgated, no convictions outraged. It could not be judged by any known standard, yet, although it was acknowledged that the supreme note of art had been struck in *The King in Yellow*, all felt that human nature could not bear the strain, nor thrive on words in which the essence of purest poison lurked. The very banality and innocence of the first act only allowed the blow to fall afterward with more awful effect.

It was, I remember, the 13th day of April, 1920, that the first Government Lethal Chamber was established on the south side of Washington Square, between Wooster Street and South Fifth Avenue. The block which had formerly consisted of a lot of shabby old buildings, used as cafés and restaurants for foreigners, had been acquired by the Government in the winter of 1898. The French and Italian cafés and restaurants were torn down; the whole block was enclosed by a gilded iron railing, and converted

into a lovely garden with lawns, flowers and fountains. In the centre of the garden stood a small, white building, severely classical in architecture, and surrounded by thickets of flowers. Six Ionic columns supported the roof, and the single door was of bronze. A splendid marble group of the "Fates" stood before the door, the work of a young American sculptor, Boris Yvain, who had died in Paris when only twenty-three years old.

The inauguration ceremonies were in progress as I crossed University Place and entered the square. I threaded my way through the silent throng of spectators, but was stopped at Fourth Street by a cordon of police. A regiment of United States lancers were drawn up in a hollow square round the Lethal Chamber. On a raised tribune facing Washington Park stood the Governor of New York, and behind him were grouped the Mayor of New York and Brooklyn, the Inspector-General of Police, the Commandant of the state troops, Colonel Livingston, military aid to the President of the United States, General Blount, commanding at Governor's Island, Major-General Hamilton, commanding the garrison of New York and Brooklyn, Admiral Buffby of the fleet in the North River, Surgeon-General Lanceford, the staff of the National Free Hospital, Senators Wyse and Franklin of New York, and the Commissioner of Public Works. The tribune was surrounded by a squadron of hussars of the National Guard.

The Governor was finishing his reply to the short speech of the Surgeon-General. I heard him say: "The laws prohibiting suicide and providing punishment for any attempt at self-destruction have been repealed. The Government has seen fit to acknowledge the right of man to end an existence which may have become intolerable to him, through physical suffering or mental despair. It is believed that the community will be benefited by the removal of such people from their midst. Since the passage of this law, the number of suicides in the United States has not increased. Now the Government has determined to establish a Lethal Chamber in every city, town and village in the country, it remains to be seen whether or not that class of human creatures from whose desponding ranks new victims of self-destruction fall daily will accept the relief thus provided." He paused, and turned to the white Lethal Chamber. The silence in the street was absolute. "There a painless death awaits him who can no longer bear the sorrows of this life. If death is welcome let him seek it there." Then quickly turning to the military aid of the President's household, he said, "I declare the Lethal Chamber open," and again facing the vast crowd he cried in a clear voice: "Citizens of New York and of the United States of America, through me the Government declares the Lethal Chamber to be open."

The solemn hush was broken by a sharp cry of command, the squadron of hussars filed after the Governor's carriage, the lancers wheeled and formed along Fifth Avenue to wait for the commandant of the garrison, and the mounted police followed them. I left the crowd to gape and stare at the white marble Death Chamber, and, crossing South Fifth Avenue, walked along the western side of that thoroughfare to Bleecker Street. Then I turned to the right and stopped before a dingy shop which bore the sign:

HAWBERK, ARMOURER.

I glanced in at the doorway and saw Hawberk busy in his little shop at the end of the hall. He looked up, and catching sight of me cried in his deep, hearty voice, "Come in, Mr. Castaigne!" Constance, his daughter, rose to meet me as I crossed the threshold, and held out her pretty hand, but I saw the blush of disappointment on her cheeks, and knew that it was another Castaigne she had expected, my cousin Louis. I smiled at her confusion and complimented her on the banner she was embroidering from a coloured plate. Old Hawberk sat riveting the worn greaves of some ancient suit of armour, and the ting! ting! ting! of his little hammer sounded pleasantly in the quaint shop. Presently he dropped his hammer, and fussed about for a moment with a tiny wrench. The soft clash of the mail sent a thrill of pleasure through me. I loved to hear the music of steel brushing against steel, the mellow shock of the mallet on thigh pieces, and the jingle of chain armour. That was the only reason I went to see Hawberk. He had never interested me personally, nor did Constance, except for the fact of her being in love with Louis. This did occupy my attention, and sometimes even kept me awake at night. But I knew in my heart that all would come right, and that I should arrange their future as I expected to arrange that of my kind doctor, John Archer. However, I should never have troubled myself about visiting them just then, had it not been, as I say, that the music of the tinkling hammer had for me this strong fascination. I would sit for hours, listening and listening, and when a stray sunbeam struck the inlaid steel, the sensation it gave me was almost too keen to endure. My eyes would become fixed, dilating with a pleasure that stretched every nerve almost to breaking, until some movement of the old armourer cut off the ray of sunlight, then, still thrilling secretly, I leaned back and listened again to the sound of the polishing rag, swish! swish! rubbing rust from the rivets.

Constance worked with the embroidery over her knees, now and then pausing to examine more closely the pattern in the coloured plate from the Metropolitan Museum.

"Who is this for?" I asked.

Hawberk explained, that in addition to the treasures of armour in the Metropolitan Museum of which he had been appointed armourer, he also had charge of several collections belonging to rich amateurs. This was the missing greave of a famous suit which a client of his had traced to a little shop in Paris on the Quai d'Orsay. He, Hawberk, had negotiated for and secured the greave, and now the suit was complete. He laid down his hammer and read me the history of the suit, traced since 1450 from owner to owner until it was acquired by Thomas Stainbridge. When his superb collection was sold, this client of Hawberk's bought the suit, and since then the search for the missing greave had been pushed until it was, almost by accident, located in Paris.

"Did you continue the search so persistently without any certainty of the greave being still in existence?" I demanded.

"Of course," he replied coolly.

Then for the first time I took a personal interest in Hawberk.

"It was worth something to you," I ventured.

"No," he replied, laughing, "my pleasure in finding it was my reward."

"Have you no ambition to be rich?" I asked, smiling.

"My one ambition is to be the best armourer in the world," he answered gravely.

Constance asked me if I had seen the ceremonies at the Lethal Chamber. She herself had noticed cavalry passing up Broadway that morning, and had wished to see the inauguration, but her father wanted the banner finished, and she had stayed at his request.

"Did you see your cousin, Mr. Castaigne, there?" she asked, with the slightest tremor of her soft eyelashes.

"No," I replied carelessly. "Louis' regiment is manœuvring out in Westchester County." I rose and picked up my hat and cane.

"Are you going upstairs to see the lunatic again?" laughed old Hawberk. If Hawberk knew how I loathe that word "lunatic," he would never use it in my presence. It rouses certain feelings within me which I do not care to explain. However, I answered him quietly: "I think I shall drop in and see Mr. Wilde for a moment or two."

"Poor fellow," said Constance, with a shake of the head, "it must be hard to live alone year after year poor, crippled and almost demented. It is very good of you, Mr. Castaigne, to visit him as often as you do."

"I think he is vicious," observed Hawberk, beginning again with his hammer. I listened to the golden tinkle on the greave plates; when he had finished I replied:

"No, he is not vicious, nor is he in the least demented. His mind is a wonder chamber, from which he can extract treasures that you and I would give years of our life to acquire.'"

Hawberk laughed.

I continued a little impatiently: "He knows history as no one else could know it. Nothing, however trivial, escapes his search, and his memory is so absolute, so precise in details, that were it known in New York that such a man existed, the people could not honour him enough."

"Nonsense," muttered Hawberk, searching on the floor for a fallen rivet.

"Is it nonsense," I asked, managing to suppress what I felt, "is it nonsense when he says that the tassets and cuissards of the enamelled suit of armour commonly known as the 'Prince's Emblazoned' can be found among a mass of rusty theatrical properties, broken stoves and ragpicker's refuse in a garret in Pell Street?"

Hawberk's hammer fell to the ground, but he picked it up and asked, with a great deal of calm, how I knew that the tassets and left cuissard were missing from the "Prince's Emblazoned."

"I did not know until Mr. Wilde mentioned it to me the other day. He said they were in the garret of 998 Pell Street."

"Nonsense," he cried, but I noticed his hand trembling under his leathern apron.

"Is this nonsense too?" I asked pleasantly, "is it nonsense when Mr. Wilde continually speaks of you as the Marquis of Avonshire and of Miss Constance—"

I did not finish, for Constance had started to her feet with terror written on every feature. Hawberk looked at me and slowly smoothed his leathern apron.

"That is impossible," he observed, "Mr. Wilde may know a great many things—"

"About armour, for instance, and the 'Prince's Emblazoned,'" I interposed, smiling.

"Yes," he continued, slowly, "about armour also—may be—but he is wrong in regard to the Marquis of Avonshire, who, as you know, killed his wife's traducer years ago, and went to Australia where he did not long survive his wife."

"Mr. Wilde is wrong," murmured Constance. Her lips were blanched, but her voice was sweet and calm.

"Let us agree, if you please, that in this one circumstance Mr. Wilde is wrong," I said.

11

I CLIMBED THE THREE DILAPIDATED flights of stairs, which I had so often climbed before, and knocked at a small door at the end of the corridor. Mr. Wilde opened the door and I walked in.

When he had double-locked the door and pushed a heavy chest against it, he came and sat down beside me, peering up into my face with his little light-coloured eyes. Half a dozen new scratches covered his nose and cheeks, and the silver wires which supported his artificial ears had become displaced. I thought I had never seen him so hideously fascinating. He had no ears. The artificial ones, which now stood out at an angle from the fine wire, were his one weakness. They were made of wax and painted a shell pink, but the rest of his face was yellow. He might better have revelled in the luxury of some artificial fingers for his left hand, which was absolutely fingerless, but it seemed to cause him no inconvenience, and he was satisfied with his wax ears. He was very small, scarcely higher than a child of ten, but his arms were magnificently developed, and his thighs as thick as any athlete's. Still, the most remarkable thing about Mr. Wilde was that a man of his marvellous intelligence and knowledge should have such a head. It was flat and pointed, like the heads of many of those unfortunates whom people imprison in asylums for the weak-minded. Many called him insane, but I knew him to be as sane as I was.

I do not deny that he was eccentric; the mania he had for keeping that cat and teasing her until she flew at his face like a demon, was certainly eccentric. I never could understand why he kept the creature, nor what pleasure he found in shutting himself up in his room with this surly, vicious beast. I remember once, glancing up from the manuscript I was studying by the light of some tallow dips, and seeing Mr. Wilde squatting motionless on his high chair, his eyes fairly blazing with excitement, while the cat, which had risen from her place before the stove, came creeping across the floor right at him. Before I could move she flattened her belly to the ground, crouched, trembled, and sprang into his face. Howling and foaming they rolled over and over on the floor, scratching and clawing, until the cat screamed and fled under the cabinet, and Mr. Wilde turned over on his back, his limbs contracting and curling up like the legs of a dying spider. He *was* eccentric.

Mr. Wilde had climbed into his high chair, and, after studying my face, picked up a dog's-eared ledger and opened it.

"Henry B. Matthews," he read, "book-keeper with Whysot Whysot and Company, dealers in church ornaments. Called April 3rd. Reputation damaged on the race-track. Known as a welcher. Reputation to be repaired by August 1st. Retainer Five Dollars." He turned the page and ran his fingerless knuckles down the closely-written columns.

"P. Greene Dusenberry, Minister of the Gospel, Fairbeach, New Jersey. Reputation damaged in the Bowery. To be repaired as soon as possible. Retainer $100."

He coughed and added, "Called, April 6th."

"Then you are not in need of money, Mr. Wilde," I inquired.

"Listen," he coughed again.

"Mrs. C. Hamilton Chester, of Chester Park, New York City. Called April 7th. Reputation damaged at Dieppe, France. To be repaired by October 1st Retainer $500.

"Note.—C. Hamilton Chester, Captain U.S.S. 'Avalanche', ordered home from South Sea Squadron October 1st."

"Well," I said, "the profession of a Repairer of Reputations is lucrative."

His colourless eyes sought mine, "I only wanted to demonstrate that I was correct. You said it was impossible to succeed as a Repairer of Reputations; that even if I did succeed in certain cases it would cost me more than I would gain by it. To-day I have five hundred men in my employ, who are poorly paid, but who pursue the work with an enthusiasm which possibly may be born of fear. These men enter every shade and grade of society; some even are pillars of the most exclusive social temples; others are the prop and pride of the financial world; still others, hold undisputed sway among the 'Fancy and the Talent.' I choose them at my leisure from those who reply to my advertisements. It is easy enough, they are all cowards. I could treble the number in twenty days if I wished. So you see, those who have in their keeping the reputations of their fellow-citizens, I have in my pay."

"They may turn on you," I suggested.

He rubbed his thumb over his cropped ears, and adjusted the wax substitutes. "I think not," he murmured thoughtfully, "I seldom have to apply the whip, and then only once. Besides they like their wages."

"How do you apply the whip?" I demanded.

His face for a moment was awful to look upon. His eyes dwindled to a pair of green sparks.

"I invite them to come and have a little chat with me," he said in a soft voice.

A knock at the door interrupted him, and his face resumed its amiable expression.

"Who is it?" he inquired.

"Mr. Steylette," was the answer.

"Come to-morrow," replied Mr. Wilde.

"Impossible," began the other, but was silenced by a sort of bark from Mr. Wilde.

"Come to-morrow," he repeated.

We heard somebody move away from the door and turn the corner by the stairway.

"Who is that?" I asked.

"Arnold Steylette, Owner and Editor in Chief of the great New York daily."

He drummed on the ledger with his fingerless hand adding: "I pay him very badly, but he thinks it a good bargain."

"Arnold Steylette!" I repeated amazed.

"Yes," said Mr. Wilde, with a self-satisfied cough.

The cat, which had entered the room as he spoke, hesitated, looked up at him and snarled. He climbed down from the chair and squatting on the floor, took the creature into his arms and caressed her. The cat ceased snarling and presently began a loud purring which seemed to increase in timbre as he stroked her. "Where are the notes?" I asked. He pointed to the table, and for the hundredth time I picked up the bundle of manuscript entitled—

«THE IMPERIAL DYNASTY OF AMERICA.»

One by one I studied the well-worn pages, worn only by my own handling, and although I knew all by heart, from the beginning, "When from Carcosa, the Hyades, Hastur, and Aldebaran," to "Castaigne, Louis de Calvados, born December 19th, 1877," I read it with an eager, rapt attention, pausing to repeat parts of it aloud, and dwelling especially on "Hildred de Calvados, only son of Hildred Castaigne and Edythe Landes Castaigne, first in succession," etc., etc.

When I finished, Mr. Wilde nodded and coughed.

"Speaking of your legitimate ambition," he said, "how do Constance and Louis get along?"

"She loves him," I replied simply.

The cat on his knee suddenly turned and struck at his eyes, and he flung her off and climbed on to the chair opposite me.

"And Dr. Archer! But that's a matter you can settle any time you wish," he added.

"Yes," I replied, "Dr. Archer can wait, but it is time I saw my cousin Louis."

"It is time," he repeated. Then he took another ledger from the table and ran over the leaves rapidly. "We are now in communication with ten thousand men," he muttered. "We can count on one hundred thousand within the first twenty-eight hours, and in forty-eight hours the state will rise *en masse*. The country follows the state, and the portion that will not, I mean California and the Northwest, might better never have been inhabited. I shall not send them the Yellow Sign."

The blood rushed to my head, but I only answered, "A new broom sweeps clean."

"The ambition of Caesar and of Napoleon pales before that which could not rest until it had seized the minds of men and controlled even their unborn thoughts," said Mr. Wilde.

"You are speaking of the King in Yellow," I groaned, with a shudder.

"He is a king whom emperors have served."

"I am content to serve him," I replied.

Mr. Wilde sat rubbing his ears with his crippled hand. "Perhaps Constance does not love him," he suggested.

I started to reply, but a sudden burst of military music from the street below drowned my voice. The twentieth dragoon regiment, formerly in garrison at Mount St. Vincent, was returning from the manœuvres in Westchester County, to its new barracks on East Washington Square. It was my cousin's regiment. They were a fine lot of fellows, in their pale blue, tight-fitting jackets, jaunty busbys and white riding breeches with the double yellow stripe, into which their limbs seemed moulded. Every other squadron was armed with lances, from the metal points of which fluttered yellow and white pennons. The band passed, playing the regimental march, then came the colonel and staff, the horses crowding and trampling, while their heads bobbed in unison, and the pennons fluttered from their lance points. The troopers, who rode with the beautiful English seat, looked brown as berries from their bloodless campaign among the farms of Westchester, and the music of their sabres against the stirrups, and the jingle of spurs and carbines was delightful to me. I saw Louis riding with his squadron. He was as handsome an officer as I have ever seen. Mr. Wilde, who had mounted a chair by the window, saw him too, but said nothing. Louis turned and looked straight at Hawberk's shop as he passed, and I could see the flush on his brown cheeks. I think Constance must have been at the window. When the last troopers had clattered by, and the last pennons vanished into South Fifth Avenue, Mr. Wilde clambered out of his chair and dragged the chest away from the door.

"Yes," he said, "it is time that you saw your cousin Louis."

He unlocked the door and I picked up my hat and stick and stepped into the corridor. The stairs were dark. Groping about, I set my foot on something soft, which snarled and spit, and I aimed a murderous blow at the cat, but my cane shivered to splinters against the balustrade, and the beast scurried back into Mr. Wilde's room.

Passing Hawberk's door again I saw him still at work on the armour, but I did not stop, and stepping out into Bleecker Street, I followed it to Wooster, skirted the grounds of the Lethal Chamber, and crossing Washington Park went straight to my rooms in the Benedick. Here I lunched comfortably, read the *Herald* and the *Meteor*, and finally went to the steel safe in my bedroom and set the time combination. The three and three-quarter minutes which it is necessary to wait, while the time lock is opening, are to me golden moments. From the instant I set the combination to the moment when I grasp the knobs and swing back the solid steel doors, I live in an ecstasy of expectation. Those moments must be like moments passed in Paradise. I know what I am to find at the end of the time limit. I know what the massive safe holds secure for me, for me alone, and the exquisite pleasure of waiting is hardly enhanced when the safe opens and I lift, from its velvet crown, a diadem of purest gold, blazing with diamonds. I do this every day, and yet the joy of waiting and at last touching again the diadem, only seems to increase as the days pass. It is a diadem fit for a King among kings, an Emperor among emperors. The King in Yellow might scorn it, but it shall be worn by his royal servant.

I held it in my arms until the alarm in the safe rang harshly, and then tenderly, proudly, I replaced it and shut the steel doors. I walked slowly back into my study, which faces Washington Square, and leaned on the window sill. The afternoon sun poured into my windows, and a gentle breeze stirred the branches of the elms and maples in the park, now covered with buds and tender foliage. A flock of pigeons circled about the tower of the Memorial Church; sometimes alighting on the purple tiled roof, sometimes wheeling downward to the lotos fountain in front of the marble arch. The gardeners were busy with the flower beds around the fountain, and the freshly turned earth smelled sweet and spicy. A lawn mower, drawn by a fat white horse, clinked across the green sward, and watering-carts poured showers of spray over the asphalt drives. Around the statue of Peter Stuyvesant, which in 1897 had replaced the monstrosity supposed to represent Garibaldi, children played in the spring sunshine, and nurse girls wheeled elaborate baby carriages with a reckless disregard for the pasty-faced occupants, which could probably be explained by the presence of half a dozen trim dragoon troopers languidly lolling on the benches. Through the trees, the Washington Memorial Arch glistened like silver in the sunshine, and beyond, on the eastern extremity of the square the grey stone barracks of the dragoons, and the white granite artillery stables were alive with colour and motion.

I looked at the Lethal Chamber on the corner of the square opposite. A few curious people still lingered about the gilded iron railing, but inside the grounds the paths were deserted. I watched the fountains ripple and sparkle; the sparrows had already found this new bathing nook, and the basins were covered with the dusty-feathered little things. Two or three white peacocks picked their way across the lawns, and a drab coloured pigeon sat so motionless on the arm of one of the "Fates," that it seemed to be a part of the sculptured stone.

As I was turning carelessly away, a slight commotion in the group of curious loiterers around the gates attracted my attention. A young man had entered, and was advancing with nervous strides along the gravel path which leads to the bronze doors of the Lethal Chamber. He paused a moment before the "Fates," and as he raised his head to those three mysterious faces, the pigeon rose from its sculptured perch, circled about for a moment and wheeled to the east. The young man pressed his hand to his face, and then with an undefinable gesture sprang up the marble steps, the bronze doors closed behind him, and half an hour later the loiterers slouched away, and the frightened pigeon returned to its perch in the arms of Fate.

I put on my hat and went out into the park for a little walk before dinner. As I crossed the central driveway a group of officers passed, and one of them called out, "Hello, Hildred," and came back to shake hands with me. It was my cousin Louis, who stood smiling and tapping his spurred heels with his riding-whip.

"Just back from Westchester," he said; "been doing the bucolic; milk and curds, you know, dairy-maids in sunbonnets, who say 'haeow' and 'I don't think' when you tell them they are pretty. I'm nearly dead for a square meal at Delmonico's. What's the news?"

"There is none," I replied pleasantly. "I saw your regiment coming in this morning."

"Did you? I didn't see you. Where were you?"

"In Mr. Wilde's window."

"Oh, hell!" he began impatiently, "that man is stark mad! I don't understand why you—"

He saw how annoyed I felt by this outburst, and begged my pardon.

"Really, old chap," he said, "I don't mean to run down a man you like, but for the life of me I can't see what the deuce you find in common with Mr. Wilde. He's not well bred, to put it generously; he is hideously deformed; his head is the head of a criminally insane person. You know yourself he's been in an asylum—"

"So have I," I interrupted calmly.

Louis looked startled and confused for a moment, but recovered and slapped me heartily on the shoulder. "You were completely cured," he began; but I stopped him again.

"I suppose you mean that I was simply acknowledged never to have been insane."

"Of course that—that's what I meant," he laughed.

I disliked his laugh because I knew it was forced, but I nodded gaily and asked him where he was going. Louis looked after his brother officers who had now almost reached Broadway.

"We had intended to sample a Brunswick cocktail, but to tell you the truth I was anxious for an excuse to go and see Hawberk instead. Come along, I'll make you my excuse."

We found old Hawberk, neatly attired in a fresh spring suit, standing at the door of his shop and sniffing the air.

"I had just decided to take Constance for a little stroll before dinner," he replied to the impetuous volley of questions from Louis. "We thought of walking on the park terrace along the North River."

At that moment Constance appeared and grew pale and rosy by turns as Louis bent over her small gloved fingers. I tried to excuse myself, alleging an engagement uptown, but Louis and Constance would not listen, and I saw I was expected to remain and engage old Hawberk's attention. After all it would be just as well if I kept my eye on Louis, I thought, and when they hailed a Spring Street horse-car, I got in after them and took my seat beside the armourer.

The beautiful line of parks and granite terraces overlooking the wharves along the North River, which were built in 1910 and finished in the autumn of 1917, had become one of the most popular promenades in the metropolis. They extended from the battery to 190th Street, overlooking the noble river and affording a fine view of the Jersey shore and the Highlands opposite. Cafés and restaurants were scattered here and there among the trees, and twice a week military bands from the garrison played in the kiosques on the parapets.

We sat down in the sunshine on the bench at the foot of the equestrian statue of General Sheridan. Constance tipped her sunshade to shield her eyes, and she and Louis began a murmuring conversation which was impossible to catch. Old Hawberk, leaning on his ivory headed cane, lighted an excellent cigar, the mate to which I politely refused, and smiled at vacancy. The sun hung low above the Staten Island woods, and the bay was dyed with golden hues reflected from the sun-warmed sails of the shipping in the harbour.

Brigs, schooners, yachts, clumsy ferry-boats, their decks swarming with people, railroad transports carrying lines of brown, blue and white freight cars, stately sound steamers, déclassé tramp steamers, coasters, dredgers, scows, and everywhere pervading the entire bay impudent little tugs puffing and whistling officiously;—these were the craft which churned the sunlight waters as far as the eye could reach. In calm contrast to the hurry of sailing vessel and steamer a silent fleet of white warships lay motionless in midstream.

Constance's merry laugh aroused me from my reverie.

"What *are* you staring at?" she inquired.

"Nothing—the fleet," I smiled.

Then Louis told us what the vessels were, pointing out each by its relative position to the old Red Fort on Governor's Island.

"That little cigar shaped thing is a torpedo boat," he explained; "there are four more lying close together. They are the *Tarpon*, the *Falcon*, the *Sea Fox*, and the *Octopus*. The gun-boats just above are the *Princeton*, the *Champlain*, the *Still Water* and the *Erie*. Next to them lie the cruisers *Faragut* and *Los Angeles*, and above them the battle ships *California*, and *Dakota*, and the *Washington* which is the flag ship. Those two squatty looking chunks of metal which are anchored there off Castle William are the double turreted monitors *Terrible* and *Magnificent*; behind them lies the ram, *Osceola*."

Constance looked at him with deep approval in her beautiful eyes. "What loads of things you know for a soldier," she said, and we all joined in the laugh which followed.

Presently Louis rose with a nod to us and offered his arm to Constance, and they strolled away along the river wall. Hawberk watched them for a moment and then turned to me.

"Mr. Wilde was right," he said. "I have found the missing tassets and left cuissard of the 'Prince's Emblazoned,' in a vile old junk garret in Pell Street."

"998?" I inquired, with a smile.

"Yes."

"Mr. Wilde is a very intelligent man," I observed.

"I want to give him the credit of this most important discovery," continued Hawberk. "And I intend it shall be known that he is entitled to the fame of it."

"He won't thank you for that," I answered sharply; "please say nothing about it."

"Do you know what it is worth?" said Hawberk.

"No, fifty dollars, perhaps."

"It is valued at five hundred, but the owner of the 'Prince's Emblazoned' will give two thousand dollars to the person who completes his suit; that reward also belongs to Mr. Wilde."

"He doesn't want it! He refuses it!" I answered angrily. "What do you know about Mr. Wilde? He doesn't need the money. He is rich—or will be—richer than any living man except myself. What will we care for money then—what will we care, he and I, when—when—"

"When what?" demanded Hawberk, astonished.

"You will see," I replied, on my guard again.

He looked at me narrowly, much as Doctor Archer used to, and I knew he thought I was mentally unsound. Perhaps it was fortunate for him that he did not use the word lunatic just then.

"No," I replied to his unspoken thought, "I am not mentally weak; my mind is as healthy as Mr. Wilde's. I do not care to explain just yet what I have on hand, but it is an investment which will pay more than mere gold, silver and precious stones. It will secure the happiness and prosperity of a continent—yes, a hemisphere!"

"Oh," said Hawberk.

"And eventually," I continued more quietly, "it will secure the happiness of the whole world."

"And incidentally your own happiness and prosperity as well as Mr. Wilde's?"

"Exactly," I smiled. But I could have throttled him for taking that tone.

He looked at me in silence for a while and then said very gently, "Why don't you give up your books and studies, Mr. Castaigne, and take a tramp among the mountains somewhere or other? You used to be fond of fishing. Take a cast or two at the trout in the Rangelys."

"I don't care for fishing any more," I answered, without a shade of annoyance in my voice.

"You used to be fond of everything," he continued; "athletics, yachting, shooting, riding—"

"I have never cared to ride since my fall," I said quietly.

"Ah, yes, your fall," he repeated, looking away from me.

I thought this nonsense had gone far enough, so I brought the conversation back to Mr. Wilde; but he was scanning my face again in a manner highly offensive to me.

"Mr. Wilde," he repeated, "do you know what he did this afternoon? He came downstairs and nailed a sign over the hall door next to mine; it read:

MR. WILDE,
REPAIRER OF REPUTATIONS.
Third Bell.

"Do you know what a Repairer of Reputations can be?"

"I do," I replied, suppressing the rage within.

"Oh," he said again.

Louis and Constance came strolling by and stopped to ask if we would join them. Hawberk looked at his watch. At the same moment a puff of smoke shot from the casemates of Castle William, and the boom of the sunset gun rolled across the water and was re-echoed from the Highlands opposite. The flag came running down from the flag-pole, the bugles sounded on the white decks of the warships, and the first electric light sparkled out from the Jersey shore.

As I turned into the city with Hawberk I heard Constance murmur something to Louis which I did not understand; but Louis whispered "My darling," in reply; and again, walking ahead with Hawberk through the square I heard a murmur of "sweetheart," and "my own Constance," and I knew the time had nearly arrived when I should speak of important matters with my cousin Louis.

III

ONE MORNING EARLY IN MAY I STOOD before the steel safe in my bedroom, trying on the golden jewelled crown. The diamonds flashed fire as I turned to the mirror, and the heavy beaten gold burned like a halo about my head. I remembered Camilla's agonized scream and the awful words echoing through the dim streets of Carcosa. They were the last lines in the first act, and I dared not think of what followed—dared not, even in the spring sunshine, there in my own room, surrounded with familiar objects, reassured by the bustle from the street and the voices of the servants in the hallway outside. For those poisoned words had dropped slowly into my heart, as death-sweat drops upon a bed-sheet and is absorbed. Trembling, I put the diadem from my head and wiped my forehead, but I thought of Hastur and of my own rightful ambition, and I remembered Mr. Wilde as I had last left him, his face all torn and bloody from the claws of that devil's creature, and what he said—ah, what he said. The alarm bell in the safe began to whirr harshly, and I knew my time was up; but I would not heed it, and replacing the flashing circlet upon my head I turned defiantly to the mirror. I stood for a long time absorbed in the changing expression of my own eyes. The mirror reflected a face which was like my own, but whiter, and so thin that I hardly recognized it. And all the time I kept repeating between my clenched teeth, "The day has come! the day has come!" while the alarm in the safe whirred and clamoured, and the diamonds sparkled and flamed above my brow. I heard a door open but did not heed it. It was only when I saw two faces in the mirror:—it was only when another face rose over my shoulder, and two other eyes met mine. I wheeled like a flash and seized a long knife from my dressing-table, and my cousin sprang back very pale, crying: "Hildred! for God's sake!" then as my hand fell, he said: "It is I, Louis, don't you know me?" I stood silent. I could not have spoken for my life. He walked up to me and took the knife from my hand.

"What is all this?" he inquired, in a gentle voice. "Are you ill?"

"No," I replied. But I doubt if he heard me.

"Come, come, old fellow," he cried, "take off that brass crown and toddle into the study. Are you going to a masquerade? What's all this theatrical tinsel anyway?"

I was glad he thought the crown was made of brass and paste, yet I didn't like him any the better for thinking so. I let him take it from my hand, knowing it was best to humour him. He tossed the splendid diadem in the air, and catching it, turned to me smiling.

"It's dear at fifty cents," he said. "What's it for?"

I did not answer, but took the circlet from his hands, and placing it in the safe shut the massive steel door. The alarm ceased its infernal din at once. He watched me curiously, but did not seem to notice the sudden ceasing of the alarm. He did, however, speak of the safe as a biscuit box. Fearing lest he might examine the combination I led the way into my study. Louis threw himself on the sofa and flicked at flies with his eternal riding-whip. He wore his fatigue uniform with the braided jacket and jaunty cap, and I noticed that his riding-boots were all splashed with red mud.

"Where have you been?" I inquired.

"Jumping mud creeks in Jersey," he said. "I haven't had time to change yet; I was rather in a hurry to see you. Haven't you got a glass of something? I'm dead tired; been in the saddle twenty-four hours."

I gave him some brandy from my medicinal store, which he drank with a grimace.

"Damned bad stuff," he observed. "I'll give you an address where they sell brandy that is brandy."

"It's good enough for my needs," I said indifferently. "I use it to rub my chest with." He stared and flicked at another fly.

"See here, old fellow," he began, "I've got something to suggest to you. It's four years now that you've shut yourself up here like an owl, never going anywhere, never taking any healthy exercise, never doing a damn thing but poring over those books up there on the mantelpiece."

He glanced along the row of shelves. "Napoleon, Napoleon, Napoleon!" he read. "For heaven's sake, have you nothing but Napoleons there?"

"I wish they were bound in gold," I said. "But wait, yes, there is another book, *The King in Yellow*." I looked him steadily in the eye.

"Have you never read it?" I asked.

"I? No, thank God! I don't want to be driven crazy."

I saw he regretted his speech as soon as he had uttered it. There is only one word which I loathe more than I do lunatic and that word is crazy. But I controlled myself and asked him why he thought *The King in Yellow* dangerous.

"Oh, I don't know," he said, hastily. "I only remember the excitement it created and the denunciations from pulpit and Press. I believe the author shot himself after bringing forth this monstrosity, didn't he?"

"I understand he is still alive," I answered.

"That's probably true," he muttered; "bullets couldn't kill a fiend like that."

"It is a book of great truths," I said.

"Yes," he replied, "of 'truths' which send men frantic and blast their lives. I don't care if the thing is, as they say, the very supreme essence of art. It's a crime to have written it, and I for one shall never open its pages."

"Is that what you have come to tell me?" I asked.

"No," he said, "I came to tell you that I am going to be married."

I believe for a moment my heart ceased to beat, but I kept my eyes on his face.

"Yes," he continued, smiling happily, "married to the sweetest girl on earth."

"Constance Hawberk," I said mechanically.

"How did you know?" he cried, astonished. "I didn't know it myself until that evening last April, when we strolled down to the embankment before dinner."

"When is it to be?" I asked.

"It was to have been next September, but an hour ago a despatch came ordering our regiment to the Presidio, San Francisco. We leave at noon to-morrow. To-morrow," he repeated. "Just think, Hildred, to-morrow I shall be the happiest fellow that ever drew breath in this jolly world, for Constance will go with me."

I offered him my hand in congratulation, and he seized and shook it like the good-natured fool he was—or pretended to be.

"I am going to get my squadron as a wedding present," he rattled on. "Captain and Mrs. Louis Castaigne, eh, Hildred?"

Then he told me where it was to be and who were to be there, and made me promise to come and be best man. I set my teeth and listened to his boyish chatter without showing what I felt, but—

I was getting to the limit of my endurance, and when he jumped up, and, switching his spurs till they jingled, said he must go, I did not detain him.

"There's one thing I want to ask of you," I said quietly.

"Out with it, it's promised," he laughed.

"I want you to meet me for a quarter of an hour's talk to-night."

"Of course, if you wish," he said, somewhat puzzled. "Where?"

"Anywhere, in the park there."

"What time, Hildred?"

"Midnight."

"What in the name of—" he began, but checked himself and laughingly assented. I watched him go down the stairs and hurry away, his sabre banging at every stride. He turned into Bleecker Street, and I knew he was going to see Constance. I gave him ten minutes to disappear and then followed in his footsteps, taking with me the jewelled crown and the silken robe embroidered with the Yellow Sign. When I turned into Bleecker Street, and entered the doorway which bore the sign—

MR. WILDE,
REPAIRER OF REPUTATIONS.
Third Bell.

I saw old Hawberk moving about in his shop, and imagined I heard Constance's voice in the parlour; but I avoided them both and hurried up the trembling stairways to Mr. Wilde's apartment. I knocked and entered without ceremony. Mr. Wilde lay groaning on the floor, his face covered with blood, his clothes torn to shreds. Drops of blood were scattered about over the carpet, which had also been ripped and frayed in the evidently recent struggle.

"It's that cursed cat," he said, ceasing his groans, and turning his colourless eyes to me; "she attacked me while I was asleep. I believe she will kill me yet."

This was too much, so I went into the kitchen, and, seizing a hatchet from the pantry, started to find the infernal beast and settle her then and there. My search was fruitless, and after a while I gave it up and came back to find Mr. Wilde squatting on his high chair by the table. He had washed his face and changed his clothes. The great furrows which the cat's claws had ploughed up in his face he had filled with collodion, and a rag hid the wound in his throat. I told him I should kill the cat when I came across her, but he only shook his head and turned to the open ledger before him. He read name after name of the people who had come to him in regard to their reputation, and the sums he had amassed were startling.

"I put on the screws now and then," he explained.

"One day or other some of these people will assassinate you," I insisted.

"Do you think so?" he said, rubbing his mutilated ears.

It was useless to argue with him, so I took down the manuscript entitled Imperial Dynasty of America, for the last time I should ever take it down in Mr. Wilde's study. I read it through, thrilling and trembling with pleasure. When I had finished Mr. Wilde took the manuscript and, turning to the dark passage which leads from his study to his bed-chamber, called out in a loud voice, "Vance." Then for the first time, I noticed a man crouching there in the shadow. How I had overlooked him during my search for the cat, I cannot imagine.

"Vance, come in," cried Mr. Wilde.

The figure rose and crept towards us, and I shall never forget the face that he raised to mine, as the light from the window illuminated it.

"Vance, this is Mr. Castaigne," said Mr. Wilde. Before he had finished speaking, the man threw himself on the ground before the table, crying and grasping, "Oh, God! Oh, my God! Help me! Forgive me! Oh, Mr. Castaigne, keep that man away. You cannot, you cannot mean it! You are different—save me! I am broken down—I was in a madhouse and now—when all was coming right—when I had forgotten the King—the King in Yellow and—but I shall go mad again—I shall go mad—"

His voice died into a choking rattle, for Mr. Wilde had leapt on him and his right hand encircled the man's throat. When Vance fell in a heap on the floor, Mr. Wilde clambered nimbly into his chair again, and rubbing his mangled ears with the stump of his hand, turned to me and asked me for the ledger. I reached it down from the shelf and he opened it. After a moment's searching among the beautifully written pages, he coughed complacently, and pointed to the name Vance.

"Vance," he read aloud, "Osgood Oswald Vance." At the sound of his name, the man on the floor raised his head and turned a convulsed face to Mr. Wilde. His eyes were injected with blood, his lips tumefied. "Called April 28th," continued Mr. Wilde. "Occupation, cashier in the Seaforth National Bank; has served a term of forgery at Sing Sing, from whence he was transferred to the Asylum for the Criminal Insane. Pardoned by the Governor of New York, and discharged from the Asylum, January 19, 1918. Reputation damaged at Sheepshead Bay. Rumours that he lives beyond his income. Reputation to be repaired at once. Retainer $1,500.

"Note.—Has embezzled sums amounting to $30,000 since March 20, 1919, excellent family, and secured present position through uncle's influence. Father, President of Seaforth Bank."

I looked at the man on the floor.

"Get up, Vance," said Mr. Wilde in a gentle voice. Vance rose as if hypnotized. "He will do as we suggest now," observed Mr. Wilde, and opening the manuscript, he read the entire history of the Imperial Dynasty of America. Then in a kind and soothing murmur he ran over the important points with Vance, who stood like one stunned. His eyes were so blank and vacant that I imagined he had become half-witted, and remarked it to Mr. Wilde who replied that it was of no consequence anyway. Very patiently we pointed out to Vance what his share in the affair would be, and he seemed to understand after a while. Mr. Wilde explained the manuscript, using several volumes on Heraldry, to substantiate the result of his researches. He mentioned the establishment of the Dynasty in Carcosa, the lakes which connected Hastur, Aldebaran and the mystery of the Hyades. He spoke of Cassilda and Camilla, and sounded the cloudy depths of Demhe, and the Lake of Hali. "The scolloped tatters of the King in Yellow must hide Yhtill forever," he muttered, but I do not believe Vance heard him. Then by degrees he led Vance along the ramifications of the Imperial family, to Uoht and Thale, from Naotalba and Phantom of Truth, to Aldones, and then tossing aside his manuscript and notes, he began the wonderful story of the Last King. Fascinated and thrilled I watched him. He threw up his head, his long arms were stretched out in a magnificent gesture of pride and power, and his eyes blazed deep in their sockets like two emeralds. Vance listened stupefied. As for me, when at last Mr. Wilde had finished, and pointing to me, cried, "The cousin of the King!" my head swam with excitement.

Controlling myself with a super-human effort, I explained to Vance why I alone was worthy of the crown and why my cousin must be exiled or die. I made him understand that my cousin must never marry, even after renouncing all his claims, and how that least of all he should marry the daughter of the Marquis of Avonshire and bring England into the question. I showed him a list of thousands of names which Mr. Wilde had drawn up; every man whose name was there had received the Yellow Sign which no living human being dared disregard. The city, the state, the whole land, were ready to rise and tremble before the Pallid Mask.

The time had come, the people should know the son of Hastur, and the whole world bow to the black stars which hang in the sky over Carcosa.

Vance leaned on the table, his head buried in his hands. Mr. Wilde drew a rough sketch on the margin of yester-day's *Herald* with a bit of lead pencil. It was a plan of Hawberk's rooms. Then he wrote out the order and affixed the seal, and shaking like a palsied man I signed my first writ of execution with my name Hildred-Rex.

Mr. Wilde clambered to the floor and unlocking the cabinet, took a long square box from the first shelf. This he brought to the table and opened. A new knife lay in the tissue paper inside and I picked it up and handed it to Vance, along with the order and the plan of Hawberk's apartment. Then Mr. Wilde told Vance he could go; and he went, shambling like an out-cast of the slums.

I sat for a while watching the day-light fade behind the square tower of the Judson Memorial Church, and finally, gathering up the manuscript and notes, took my hat and started for the door.

Mr. Wilde watched me in silence. When I had stepped into the hall I looked back. Mr. Wilde's small eyes were still fixed on me. Behind him, the shadows gathered in the fading light. Then I closed the door behind me and went out into the darkening streets.

I had eaten nothing since break-fast, but I was not hungry. A wretched, half-starved creature, who stood look-ing across the street at the Lethal Chamber, noticed me and came up to tell me a tale of misery. I gave him money, I don't know why, and he went away without thanking me. An hour later another outcast approached and whined his story. I had a blank bit of paper in my pocket, on which was traced the Yellow Sign, and I handed it to him. He looked at it stupidly for a moment, and then with an uncer-tain glance at me, folded it with what seemed to me exaggerated care and placed it in his bosom.

The electric lights were sparkling among the trees, and the new moon shone in the sky above the Lethal Chamber. It was tiresome waiting in the square; I wandered from the Marble Arch to the artillery stables and back again to the lotos fountain. The flowers and grass exhaled a fragrance which troubled me. The jet of the fountain played in the moonlight, and the musical splash of falling drops reminded me of the tinkle of chained mail in Hawberk's shop. But it was not so fascinating, and the dull sparkle of the moonlight on the water brought no such sensations of exquisite pleasure, as when the sunshine played over the polished steel of a corselet on Hawberk's knee. I watched the bats darting and turning above the water plants in the fountain basin, but their rapid, jerky flight set my nerves on edge, and I went away again to walk aimlessly to and fro among the trees.

The artillery stables were dark, but in the cavalry barracks the officers' windows were brilliantly lighted, and the sallyport was constantly filled with troopers in fatigue, carrying straw and harness and baskets filled with tin dishes.

Twice the mounted sentry at the gates was changed while I wandered up and down the asphalt walk. I looked at my watch. It was nearly time. The lights in the barracks went out one by one, the barred gate was closed, and every minute or two an officer passed in through the side wicket, leaving a rattle of accoutrements and a jingle of spurs on the night air. The square had become very silent. The last homeless loiterer had been driven away by the grey-coated park policeman, the car tracks along Wooster Street were deserted, and the only sound which broke the stillness was the stamping of the sentry's horse and the ring of his sabre against the saddle pommel. In the barracks, the officers' quarters were still lighted, and military servants passed and repassed before the bay windows. Twelve o'clock sounded from the new spire of St. Francis Xavier, and at the last stroke of the sad-toned bell a figure passed through the wicket beside the portcullis, returned the salute of the sentry, and crossing the street entered the square and advanced toward the Benedick apartment house.

"Louis," I called.

The man pivoted on his spurred heels and came straight toward me.

"Is that you, Hildred?"

"Yes, you are on time."

I took his offered hand, and we strolled toward the Lethal Chamber.

He rattled on about his wedding and the graces of Constance, and their future prospects, calling my attention to his captain's shoulder-straps, and the triple gold arabesque on his sleeve and fatigue cap. I believe I listened as much to the music of his spurs and sabre as I did to his boyish babble, and at last we stood under the elms on the Fourth Street corner of the square opposite the Lethal Chamber. Then he laughed and asked me what I wanted with him. I motioned him to a seat on a bench under the electric light, and sat down beside him. He looked at me curiously, with that same searching glance which I hate and fear so in doctors. I felt the insult of his look, but he did not know it, and I carefully concealed my feelings.

"Well, old chap," he inquired, "what can I do for you?"

I drew from my pocket the manuscript and notes of the Imperial Dynasty of America, and looking him in the eye said:

"I will tell you. On your word as a soldier, promise me to read this manuscript from beginning to end, without asking me a question. Promise me to read these notes in the same way, and promise me to listen to what I have to tell later."

"I promise, if you wish it," he said pleasantly. "Give me the paper, Hildred."

He began to read, raising his eyebrows with a puzzled, whimsical air, which made me tremble with suppressed anger. As he advanced his, eyebrows contracted, and his lips seemed to form the word "rubbish."

Then he looked slightly bored, but apparently for my sake read, with an attempt at interest, which presently ceased to be an effort. He started when in the closely written pages he came to his own name, and when he came to mine he lowered the paper, and looked sharply at me for a moment. But he kept his word, and resumed his reading, and I let the half-formed question die on his lips unanswered. When he came to the end and read the signature of Mr. Wilde, he folded the paper carefully and returned it to me. I handed him the notes, and he settled back, pushing his fatigue cap up to his forehead, with a boyish gesture, which I remembered so well in school. I watched his face as he read, and when he finished I took the notes with the manuscript, and placed them in my pocket. Then I unfolded a scroll marked with the Yellow Sign. He saw the sign, but he did not seem to recognize it, and I called his attention to it somewhat sharply.

"Well," he said, "I see it. What is it?"

"It is the Yellow Sign," I said angrily.

"Oh, that's it, is it?" said Louis, in that flattering voice, which Doctor Archer used to employ with me, and would probably have employed again, had I not settled his affair for him.

I kept my rage down and answered as steadily as possible, "Listen, you have engaged your word?"

"I am listening, old chap," he replied soothingly.

I began to speak very calmly.

"Dr. Archer, having by some means become possessed of the secret of the Imperial Succession, attempted to deprive me of my right, alleging that because of a fall from my horse four years ago, I had become mentally deficient. He presumed to place me under restraint in his own house in hopes of either driving me insane or poisoning me. I have not forgotten it. I visited him last night and the interview was final."

Louis turned quite pale, but did not move. I resumed triumphantly, "There are yet three people to be interviewed in the interests of Mr. Wilde and myself. They are my cousin Louis, Mr. Hawberk, and his daughter Constance."

Louis sprang to his feet and I arose also, and flung the paper marked with the Yellow Sign to the ground.

"Oh, I don't need that to tell you what I have to say," I cried, with a laugh of triumph. "You must renounce the crown to me, do you hear, to *me*."

Louis looked at me with a startled air, but recovering himself said kindly, "Of course I renounce the—what is it I must renounce?"

"The crown," I said angrily.

"Of course," he answered, "I renounce it. Come, old chap, I'll walk back to your rooms with you."

"Don't try any of your doctor's tricks on me," I cried, trembling with fury. "Don't act as if you think I am insane."

"What nonsense," he replied. "Come, it's getting late, Hildred."

"No," I shouted, "you must listen. You cannot marry, I forbid it. Do you hear? I forbid it. You shall renounce the crown, and in reward I grant you exile, but if you refuse you shall die."

He tried to calm me, but I was roused at last, and drawing my long knife barred his way.

Then I told him how they would find Dr. Archer in the cellar with his throat open, and I laughed in his face when I thought of Vance and his knife, and the order signed by me.

"Ah, you are the King," I cried, "but I shall be King. Who are you to keep me from Empire over all the habitable earth! I was born the cousin of a king, but I shall be King!"

Louis stood white and rigid before me. Suddenly a man came running up Fourth Street, entered the gate of the Lethal Temple, traversed the path to the bronze doors at full speed, and plunged into the death chamber with the cry of one demented, and I laughed until I wept tears, for I had recognized Vance, and knew that Hawberk and his daughter were no longer in my way.

"Go," I cried to Louis, "you have ceased to be a menace. You will never marry Constance now, and if you marry any one else in your exile, I will visit you as I did my doctor last night. Mr. Wilde takes charge of you to-morrow." Then I turned and darted into South Fifth Avenue, and with a cry of terror Louis dropped his belt and sabre and followed me like the wind. I heard him close behind me at the corner of Bleecker Street, and I dashed into the doorway under Hawberk's sign. He cried, "Halt, or I fire!" but when he saw that I flew up the stairs leaving Hawberk's shop below, he left me, and I heard him hammering and shouting at their door as though it were possible to arouse the dead.

Mr. Wilde's door was open, and I entered crying, "It is done, it is done! Let the nations rise and look upon their King!" but I could not find Mr. Wilde, so I went to the cabinet and took the splendid diadem from its case. Then I drew on the white silk robe, embroidered with the Yellow Sign, and placed the crown upon my head. At last I was King, King by my right in Hastur, King because I knew the mystery of the Hyades, and my mind had sounded the depths of the Lake of Hali. I was King! The first grey pencillings of dawn would raise a tempest which would shake two hemispheres. Then as I stood, my every nerve pitched to the highest tension, faint with the joy and splendour of my thought, without, in the dark passage, a man groaned.

I seized the tallow dip and sprang to the door. The cat passed me like a demon, and the tallow dip went out, but my long knife flew swifter than she, and I heard her screech, and I knew that my knife had found her. For a moment I listened to her tumbling and thumping about in the darkness, and then when her frenzy ceased, I lighted a lamp and raised it over my head. Mr. Wilde lay on the floor with his throat torn open. At first I thought he was dead, but as I looked, a green sparkle came into his sunken eyes, his mutilated hand trembled, and then a spasm stretched his mouth from ear to ear. For a moment my terror and despair gave place to hope, but as I bent over him his eyeballs rolled clean around in his head, and he died. Then while I stood, transfixed with rage and despair, seeing my crown, my empire, every hope and every ambition, my very life, lying prostrate there with the dead master, *they* came, seized me from behind, and bound me until my veins stood out like cords, and my voice failed with the paroxysms of my frenzied screams. But I still raged, bleeding and infuriated among them, and more than one policeman felt my sharp teeth. Then when I could no longer move they came nearer; I saw old Hawberk, and behind him my cousin Louis' ghastly face, and farther away, in the corner, a woman, Constance, weeping softly.

"Ah! I see it now!" I shrieked. "You have seized the throne and the empire. Woe! woe to you who are crowned with the crown of the King in Yellow!"

[EDITOR'S NOTE.—MR. CASTAIGNE died yesterday in the Asylum for Criminal Insane.]

THE END

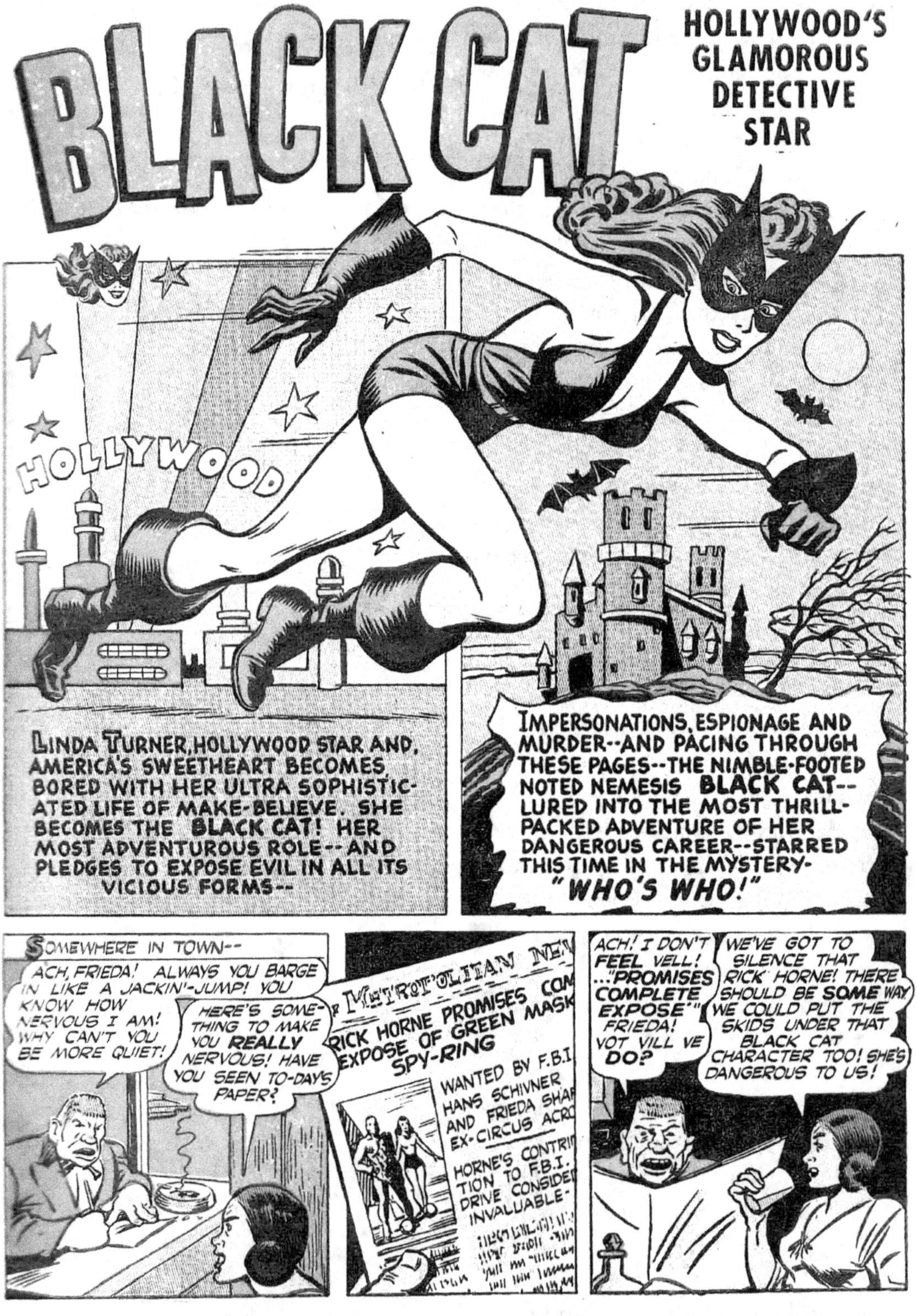

BLACK CAT

HOLLYWOOD'S GLAMOROUS DETECTIVE STAR

JA! JA! BUT THAT ISS EASIER SAID THAN DID!
WAIT, HANS--I HAVE AN IDEA! MAYBE WE CAN KILL TWO BIRDS WITH ONE STONE! LISTEN....
THAT EVENING--
SURE, AN' WHAT AN AWFUL WAY FOR A MAN TO MAKE A LIVIN'--WALK, WALK, WALK, BEGORRA, I DON'T KNOW WHAT KEEPS M'ARCHES UP! M'M--WHAT'S THAT? SOUNDS LIKE SOMEONE'S IN THE ALLEY!
WELL, BY GEORGE! AN' WHAT MIGHT YOU BE DOIN'? HAVIN' YOUR-SELF A MASQUE-RADE PARTY?
GLAD YOU DROPPED BY, COPPER- I'M HAVIN' MY-SELF A WAKE, AN' I CAN USE A CORPSE FOR THE OCCASION!
ARRGHHHH-H
THERE'LL BE SOME COMPANY FOR YOU IN A MOMENT, FLATFOOT SO YOU WON'T DIE ALONE!
RICK HORNE'S APARTMENT--
AHA! THE GUESTS ARE BEGINNING TO ARRIVE.
WELL, I'LL BE--! MY FELINE FRIEND! I DIDN'T EXPECT YOU!
I SHOULD HOPE NOT! NOT WITH THAT GAT IN YOUR MITT!
NO. I WAS EXPECTING SOME MEMBERS OF THE GREEN MASK GANG TO COME CALLING.
YES--I READ ABOUT YOUR COMING EXPOSE DARLING--THOUGHT MAYBE I COULD LEND YOU A HAND.

THAT'S MIGHTY WHITE OF YOU, BLACKIE, BUT I REALLY HAVEN'T ANY DOPE ON THAT GREEN MASK GANG....I PRINTED A FALSE LEAD IN THE PAPER AS A COME-ON. FIGURED IF THEY THOUGHT I KNEW SOMETHING THEY'D LOOK ME UP--
--THEN YOU COULD GET A LEAD ON THEM, EH? WELL, THAT'S A DIFFERENT ANGLE. I'LL TAKE A POWDER NOW--IF ANYTHING COMES UP, LET ME KNOW.
YEAH, SURE!
WHERE DID THE BLACK CAT PICK UP THAT SLANG? AND I NEVER SAW HER SMOKE BEFORE!
SOMETHING'S WRONG HERE-- I THINK I'D BETTER BAIT A HOOK!
WHAT'S COME OVER YOU, BABY? YOU'RE NOT LEAVING WITHOUT GIVING ME MY CUSTOMARY GOOD-NIGHT KISS?
OH, IS THAT CUSTOMARY!
'MMM-MMM--- HOW COULD I FORGET ANYTHING AS ENJOYABLE AS THIS!
HOLY COW! THIS ISN'T BLACK CAT! THIS IS DRACULA'S SISTER!
AND NOW, DARLING-- YOU MUST EXCUSE ME. HEY! LET GO, YOU LUG!
NIX, SISTER-- UNTIL I FIND OUT WHY YOU'RE IMPERSONATING THE BLACK CAT!
JUST WHEN I'M GETTING TO LIKE YOU, YOU GOTTA GO AND SPOIL THINGS!!
HEY!
I DON'T, AS A RULE, STRIKE WOMEN, BUT I'M GOING TO MAKE AN EXCEPTION IN YOUR CASE!!
NOW, NOW-- GOOD-LOOKING-- DON'T LET'S PLAY ROUGH!
I CAN'T BEAR TO PART WITH YOU, SISTER!
OKAY! YOU ASKED FOR IT!

JUST LIKE THE OLD DAYS-- AND NO NET!
YEOW!
AH! I'M GLAD HE DIDN'T BREAK HIS NECK! HE'S DOWNRIGHT CUTE, AND ANYWAY HE DOESN'T KNOW ANYTHING!
OKAY, SISTER--YOU WIN THIS ROUND, BUT YOU'LL BE TAKING THE COUNT IN THE NEXT ONE WHEN THE FEDS GET MY DOPE ON YOUR GANG OF SPIES!
WHY THAT-- HE WAS FOOLING ME! HE KNEW ALL THE TIME! NOW, I'VE GOT TO KILL HIM!
HA! I THOUGHT THAT WOULD GET HER!
PARDON ME, MISTER!
S'QUITE ALL RI'' OL' BOY, OL' BOY (HIC)!
WHICH WAY DID HE GO?
WHY (HIC)-- HE WEN' THAT WAY!
BANG
BANG
H'MMM-MM (HIC)?
HE COULDN'T HAVE GONE FAR!
CITY HOSHPITAL? SEN' AMB'LANSH TO PICK ME UP-- I'M NUTSH!
SWELL! NOW I'M FOLLOWING YOU, SISTER!

HE GOT AWAY! I'D BETTER SCRAM ACROSS THE ROOF BEFORE EVERY COP IN TOWN COMES SWARMING DOWN ON ME!
THAT DAME MUST BE FRIEDA SHAFFER, THE ACROBAT! SHE'S A HANDFUL OF DYNAMITE!
GONE! VANISHED INTO THIN AIR! WELL -- I'LL BE --
THE FOLLOWING MORNING, ON THE STUDIO LOT, LINDA TURNER -- FAMOUS HOLLYWOOD STAR....
THAT'S MY CUE IS RIGHT!
BUT MISS TURNER, WHERE ARE YOU GOING? THE SCENE ISN'T OVER!
WHAT ON EARTH--? "BLACK CAT KILLS POLICEMAN--- ATTEMPTS SLAYING RICK HORNE, NEWSPAPER REPORTER!" WHY, I NEVER---
THAT'S YOUR CUE, MISS TURNER!
THEN---
WHAT--?!
A LITTLE LATER, RICK HORNE RECEIVES ANOTHER VISITOR!
I'LL SOON FIND OUT WHAT... THIS IS ABOUT!

WELCOME TO MY PARLOR SAID THE DOG TO THE CAT!
RICK HORNE--! WHAT IS THE MEANING OF THIS? YOU LET ME DOWN AT ONCE!
I'VE TAKEN MORE PRECAUTIONS THIS TIME-- NOW I'M GOING TO UNMASK YOU!
LET ME DOWN!
SUDDENLY---
OUCH!
ZO! NO WONDER MEIN FRIEDA DID NOT RETURN LAST NIGHT! YOU TURNED DER TABLES ON HER!
SMACK
I'LL TURN A TABLE ON YOU, TOO-- AAAGHRR
I FINISH DER JOB SHE STARTED!
N-NO!
BANG BANG BANG
COME, FRIEDA, VE MUST GEDT AVAY FROM HERE QVICK!!
Y-YES (SOB) OF COURSE!
YOU NAZI MURDERER! YOU'LL PAY FOR THIS!
ACH, FRIEDA--YOU ARE CRYING! DER AMERICAN DOG TORTURED YOU FOR INFORMATION, JA!
WHAT--? OH, YES...
VELL, HERE VE ARE! VE DONE A GOOT DAY'S VORK, KNOCKING OFF DOT REPORTER UND GEDDING DER COPS AFTER DER BLACK CAT!
HELLO BOYS! I FIND HER ALL RIGHT-- EVERYTHING ISS OKAY!
YOU KILL REPORTER?
NO HE KILL REPORTER---

AND NOW I'M GOING TO DO MY BEST TO KILL YOU!
AIEEE
HIMMEL! VOT ISS!
FRIEDA! HAF YOU GONE CRA-- YAAAGH!
BEHOLD! HONORABLE FRAULEIN GONE BERSERK!
BUT HOW? I SAW HIM SHOOT YOU!
I WAS PREPARED FOR THE FIREWORKS! I'M WEARING A BULLET PROOF VEST! I PRETENDED I WAS SHOT SO I COULD FOLLOW YOU TWO--AND I DID, BY RIDING ON THE REAR BUMPER! SINCE YOU'RE THE REAL BLACK CAT, WHAT HAPPENED TO YOUR IMPERSONATOR?
TEN MINUTES LATER-- OUTSIDE RICK'S APARTMENT HOUSE--
RILEY! WHAT'S GOING ON HERE?
OH, MR. HORNE! THERE'S A DEAD DAME IN THE AIR-SHAFT!
RICK! YOU'RE ALIVE!
YEAH, BUT YOU WON'T BE ABLE TO SAY THE SAME FOR THESE GENTLEMEN!
AIE-EE-ARRGH
BANG
KS-01B
THE NEXT DAY-- MAYBE THE BLACK CAT HAS NINE LIVES AFTER ALL---I HOPE SO!
SAY, CASEY, ARE THERE TWO BLACK CATS?
FAITH, YOU GOT ME, MULLIGAN!
THAT'S FRIEDA SHAFFER-- OF THE GREEN-MASK GANG--
SHE MUST HAVE TRIPPED DOWN THE SHAFT WHEN I WAS CHASING HER, AND AM I GLAD SHE ISN'T THE REAL BLACK CAT! WHEW!
TOWN NEWS
BLACK CAT EXONERATED OF MURDER CHARGE AS SHE AND RICK HORNE BREAK UP THE GREEN MASK SPY RING.
GLAMOROUS, TERRIFIC BLACK CAT APPEARS REGULARLY IN EVERY HIT PARADE ISSUE OF BLACK CAT COMICS.

THE BRIDGE OF SAN LUIS REY

BY THORNTON WILDER

PART ONE:
PERHAPS AN ACCIDENT

On Friday noon, July the twentieth, 1714, the finest bridge in all Peru broke and precipitated five travellers into the gulf below. This bridge was on the highroad between Lima and Cuzco and hundreds of persons passed over it every day. It had been woven of osier by the Incas more than a century before and visitors to the city were always led out to see it. It was a mere ladder of thin slats swung out over the gorge, with handrails of dried vine. Horses and coaches and chairs had to go down hundreds of feet below and pass over the narrow torrent on rafts, but no one, not even the Viceroy, not even the Archbishop of Lima, had descended with the baggage rather than cross by the famous bridge of San Luis Rey. St. Louis of France himself protected it, by his name and by the little mud church on the further side. The bridge seemed to be among the things that last forever; it was unthinkable that it should break. The moment a Peruvian heard of the accident he signed himself and made a mental calculation as to how recently he had crossed by it and how

soon he had intended crossing by it again. People wandered about in a trance-like state, muttering; they had the hallucination of seeing themselves falling into a gulf.

There was a great service in the Cathedral. The bodies of the victims were approximately collected and approximately separated from one another, and there was great searching of hearts in the beautiful city of Lima. Servant girls returned bracelets which they had stolen from their mistresses, and usurers harangued their wives angrily, in defense of usury. Yet it was rather strange that this event should have so impressed the Limeans, for in that country those catastrophes which lawyers shockingly call the "acts of God" were more than usually frequent. Tidal waves were continually washing away cities; earthquakes arrived every week and towers fell upon good men and women all the time. Diseases were forever flitting in and out of the provinces and old age carried away some of the most admirable citizens. That is why it was so surprising that the Peruvians should have been especially touched by the rent in the bridge of San Luis Rey.

Everyone was very deeply impressed, but only one person did anything about it, and that was Brother Juniper. By a series of coincidences so extraordinary that one almost suspects the presence of some Intention, this little red-haired Franciscan from Northern Italy happened to be in Peru converting the Indians and happened to witness the accident.

It was a very hot noon, that fatal noon, and coming around the shoulder of a hill Brother Juniper stopped to wipe his forehead and to gaze upon the screen of snowy peaks in the distance, then into the gorge below him filled with the dark plumage of green trees and green birds and traversed by its ladder of osier. Joy was in him; things were not going badly. He had opened several little abandoned churches and the Indians were crawling in to early Mass and groaning at the moment of miracle as though their hearts would break. Perhaps it was the pure air from the snows before him; perhaps it was the memory that brushed him for a moment of the poem that bade him raise his eyes to the helpful hills. At all events he felt at peace. Then his glance fell upon the bridge, and at that moment a twanging noise filled the air, as when the string of some musical instrument snaps in a disused room, and he saw the bridge divide and fling five gesticulating ants into the valley below.

Anyone else would have said to himself with secret joy: "Within ten minutes myself...!" But it was another thought that visited Brother Juniper: "Why did thin happen to *those* five?"

If there were any plan in the universe at all, if there were any pattern in a human life, surely it could be discovered mysteriously latent in those lives so suddenly cut off. Either we live by accident and die by accident, or we live by plan and die by plan, And on that instant Brother Juniper made the resolve to inquire into the secret lives of those five persons, that moment falling through the air, and to surprise the reason of their taking off.

It seemed to Brother Juniper that it was high time for theology to take its place among the exact sciences and he had long intended putting it there. What he had lacked hitherto was a laboratory. Oh, there had never been any lack of specimens; any number of his charges had met calamity,—spiders had stung them; their lungs had been touched; their houses had burned down and things had happened to their children from which one averts the mind. But these occasions of human woe had never been quite fit for scientific examination. They had lacked what our good savants were later to call *proper control.* The accident had been dependent upon human error, for example, or had contained elements of probability. But this collapse of the bridge of San Luis Rey was a sheer Act of God. It afforded a perfect laboratory. Here at last one could surprise His intentions in a pure state.

You and I can see that coming from anyone but Brother Juniper this plan would be the flower of a perfect skepticism. It resembled the effort of those presumptuous souls who wanted to walk on the pavements of Heaven and built the Tower of Babel to get there. But to our Franciscan there was no element of doubt in the experiment. He knew the answer. He merely wanted to prove it, historically, mathematically, to his converts,— poor obstinate converts, so slow to believe that their pains were inserted into their lives for their own good. People were always asking for good sound proofs; doubt springs eternal in the human breast, even in countries where the Inquisition can read your very thoughts in your eyes.

This was not the first time that Brother Juniper had tried to resort to such methods. Often on the long trips he had to make (scurrying from parish to parish, his robe tucked up about his knees, for haste) he would fall to dreaming of experiments that justify the ways of God to man. For instance, a complete record of the Prayers for Rain and their results. Often he had stood on the steps of one of his little churches, his flock kneeling before him on the baked street. Often he had stretched his arms to the sky and declaimed the splendid ritual. Not often, but several times, he had felt the virtue enter him and seen the little cloud forming on the horizon. But there were many times when weeks went by ... but why think of them? It was not himself he was trying to convince that rain and drought were wisely apportioned.

Thus it was that the determination rose within him at the moment of the accident. It prompted him to busy himself for six years, knocking at all the doors in Lima, asking thousands of questions, filling scores of notebooks, in his effort at establishing the fact that each of the five lost lives was a perfect whole. Everyone knew that he was working on some sort of memorial of the accident and everyone was very helpful and misleading. A few even knew the principal aim of his activity and there were patrons in high places.

The result of all this diligence was an enormous book, which as we shall see later, was publicly burned on a beautiful Spring morning in the great square. But there was a secret copy and after a great many years and without much notice it found its way to the library of the University of San Marco. There it lies between two great wooden covers collecting dust in a cupboard. It deals with one after another of the victims of the accident, cataloguing thousands of little facts and anecdotes and testimonies, and concluding with a dignified passage describing why God had settled upon that person and upon that day for His demonstration of wisdom. Yet for all his diligence Brother Juniper never knew the central passion of Doña María's life; nor of Uncle Pio's, not even of Esteban's. And I, who claim to know so much more, isn't it possible that even I have missed the very spring within the spring?

Some say that we shall never know and that to the gods we are like the flies that the boys kill on a summer day, and some say, on the contrary, that the very sparrows do not lose a feather that has not been brushed away by the finger of God.

PART TWO:
THE MARQUESA DE MONTEMAYOR

ANY Spanish schoolboy is required to know today more about Doña María, Marquesa de Montemayor, than Brother Juniper was to discover in years of research. Within a century of her death her letters had become one of the monuments of Spanish literature and her life and times have ever since been the object of long studies. But her biographers have erred in one direction as greatly as the Franciscan did in another; they have tried to invest her with a host of graces, to read back into her life and person some of the beauties that abound in her letters, whereas all real knowledge of this wonderful woman must proceed from the act of humiliating her and of divesting her of all beauties save one.

She was the daughter of a cloth-merchant who had acquired the money and the hatred of the Limeans within a stone's-throw of the Plaza. Her childhood was unhappy: she was ugly; she stuttered; her mother persecuted her with sarcasms in an effort to arouse some social charms and forced her to go about the town in a veritable harness of jewels. She lived alone and she thought alone. Many suitors presented themselves, but as long as she could she fought against the convention of her time and was determined to remain single. There were hysterical scenes with her mother, recriminations, screams and slamming of doors.

At last at twenty-six she found herself penned into marriage with a supercilious and ruined nobleman and the Cathedral of Lima fairly buzzed with the sneers of her guests. Still she lived alone and thought alone, and when an exquisite daughter was born to her she fastened upon her an idolatrous love. But little Clara took after her father; she was cold and intellectual. At the age of eight she was calmly correcting her mother's speech and presently regarding her with astonishment and repulsion. The frightened mother became meek and obsequious but she could not prevent herself from persecuting Doña Clara with nervous attention and a fatiguing love. Again there were hysterical recriminations, screams and slamming of doors. From the offers of marriage that fell to her, Doña Clara deliberately chose the one that required her removal to Spain. So to Spain she went, to that land from which it takes six months to receive an answer to one's letter. The leave-taking before so long a voyage became in Peru one of the formal services of the Church. The ship was blessed and as the space widened between the vessel and the beach both companies knelt and sang a hymn that never failed to sound weak and timid in all that open air. Doña Clara sailed with most admirable composure, leaving her mother to gaze after the bright ship, her hand pressing now her heart and now her mouth. Blurred and streaked became her view of the serene Pacific and the enormous clouds of pearl that hang forever motionless above it.

Left alone in Lima the Marquesa's life grew more and more inward. She became increasingly negligent in her dress and like all lonely people she talked to herself audibly. All her existence lay in the burning center of her mind. On that stage were performed endless dialogues with her daughter, impossible reconciliations, scenes eternally recommenced of remorse and forgiveness. On the street you beheld an old woman her red wig fallen a little over one ear, her left cheek angry with a leprous affection, her right with a complementary adjustment of rouge. Her chin was never dry; her lips were never still. Lima was a city of eccentrics, but even there she became its jest as she drove through the streets or shuffled up the steps of its churches. She was thought to be continuously drunk. Worse things were said of her and petitions were afloat that she be locked up. She had been denounced three times before the Inquisition. It is not impossible that she might have been burned had her son-in-law been less influential in Spain and had she not somehow collected a few friends about the viceregal court who suffered her for her oddity and her wide reading.

The distressing character of the relations between mother and daughter were further embittered by misunderstandings over money. The Condesa received a handsome allowance from her mother and frequent gifts. Doña Clara soon became the outstanding woman of intelligence at the Spanish court. All the wealth of Peru would have been insufficient to maintain her in the grandiose style she fancied for herself. Strangely enough her extravagance proceeded from one of the best traits in her nature: she regarded her friends, her servants and all the interesting people in the capital, as her children. In fact there seemed only one person in the world towards whom she did not expend herself in kind offices. Among her *protégés* was the cartographer De Blasiis (whose *Maps of the New World* was dedicated to the Marquesa de Montemayor amid the roars of the courtiers at Lima who read that she was the "*admiration of her city and a rising sun in the West*"); another was the scientist Azuarius whose treatise on the laws of hydraulics was suppressed by the Inquisition as being too exciting. For a decade the Condesa literally sustained all the arts and sciences of Spain; it was not her fault that nothing memorable was produced in that time.

About four years after Doña Clara's departure Doña María received her permission to visit Europe. On both sides the visit was anticipated with resolutions well nourished on self-reproach: the one to be patient, the other to be undemonstrative. Both failed. Each tortured the other and was on the point of losing her mind under the alternations of self-rebuke and the outbursts of passion. At length one day Doña María rose before dawn, daring no more than to kiss the door behind which her daughter was sleeping, took ship and returned to America. Henceforth letter-writing had to take the place of all the affection that could not be lived.

Hers were the letters that in an astonishing world have become the text-book of schoolboys and the ant-hill of the grammarians. Doña María would have invented her genius had she not been born with it, so necessary was it to her love that she attract the attention, perhaps the admiration, of her distant child. She forced herself to go out into society in order to cull its ridicules; she taught her eye to observe; she read the masterpieces of her language to discover its effects; she insinuated herself into the company of those who were celebrated for their conversation. Night after night in her baroque palace she wrote and rewrote the incredible pages, forcing from her despairing mind those miracles of wit and grace, those distilled chronicles of the viceregal court. We know now that her daughter barely glanced at the letters and that it is to the son-in-law that we owe their preservation.

The Marquesa would have been astonished to learn that her letters were immortal. Yet many critics have accused her of keeping one eye on posterity and point to a number of letters that have all the air of being bravura pieces. To them it seems impossible that Doña María should have put herself to the same pains to dazzle her daughter that most artists expend on dazzling the public. Like her son-in-law they misunderstood her: the Conde delighted in her letters, but he thought that when he had enjoyed the style he had extracted all their richness and intention, missing (as most readers do) the whole purport of literature, which is the notation of the heart. Style is but the faintly contemptible vessel in which the bitter liquid is recommended to the world. The Marquesa would even have been astonished to learn that her letters were very good, for such authors live always in the noble weather of their own minds and those productions which seem remarkable to us are little better than a day's routine to them.

This was the old woman who hour by hour would sit upon her balcony, her odd straw hat casting a purple shadow across her lined and yellow face. How often as she turned her pages with her gemmed hands, she would ask herself, almost with amusement, whether the constant pain at her heart had an organic seat. She wondered whether a subtle doctor cutting through to that battered throne could at last discover a sign and lifting his face to the amphitheatre cry out to his students: "This woman has suffered, and her suffering has left its mark upon the structure of her heart." This idea had so often visited her that one day she wrote it into a letter and her daughter scolded her for an introspective and for making a cult of sorrow.

The knowledge that she would never be loved in return acted upon her ideas as a tide acts upon cliffs. Her religious beliefs went first, for all she could ask of a god, or of immortality, was the gift of a place where daughters love their mothers; the other attributes of Heaven you could have for a song. Next she lost her belief in the sincerity of those about her. She secretly refused to believe that anyone (herself excepted) loved anyone. All families lived in a wasteful atmosphere of custom and kissed one another with secret indifference. She saw that the people of this world moved about in an armour of egotism, drunk with self-gazing, athirst for compliments, hearing little of what was said to them, unmoved by the accidents that befell their closest friends, in dread of all appeals that might interrupt their long communion with their own desires. These were the sons and daughters of Adam from Cathay to Peru. And when on the balcony her thoughts reached this turn, her mouth would contract with shame for she knew that she too sinned and that though her love for her daughter was vast enough to include all the colours of love, it was not without a shade of tyranny: she loved her daughter not for her daughter's sake, but for her own. She longed to free herself from this ignoble bond; but the passion was too fierce to cope with. And then on that green balcony a strange warfare would shake the hideous old lady, a singularly futile struggle against a temptation to which she would never have the opportunity of succumbing. How could she rule her daughter when her daughter saw to it that four thousand miles lay between them? Nevertheless Doña María wrestled with the ghost of her temptation and was worsted on every occasion. She wanted her daughter for herself; she wanted to hear her say: "You are the best of all possible mothers"; she longed to hear her whisper: "Forgive me."

About two years after her return from Spain there took place a series of inconspicuous events that had a great deal to tell about the inner life of the Marquesa. Only the faintest allusion to them occurs in the Correspondence, but as that is found in Letter XXII which contains other signs I shall do my best to give a translation and commentary of the first part of the letter:

«*Are there no doctors in Spain? Where are those good men from Flanders that used to help you so? Oh, my treasure, how can we punish you enough for letting your cold endure so many weeks? Don Vicente, I implore you to make my child see reason. Angels of Heaven, I implore you to make my child see reason. Now that you are better, I beg of you, resolve that when the first warning of a cold comes you will steam yourself well and go to bed. Here in Peru I am helpless; I can do nothing. Do not be self-willed, beloved. God bless you. I am enclosing in today's packet the gum of some tree which the sisters of San Tomás peddle from door to door. Whether it be of much use I know not. It can do no harm. I am told that in the convent the silly sisters inhale it so diligently that one cannot smell the incense at Mass. Whether it be worth anything I know not; try it.*

«*Rest easy, my love, I am sending His Mos. Catholic Majesty the perfect gold chain.*" (Her daughter had written her: "*The chain arrived in good condition and I wore it at the christening of the Infante. His Most Catholic Majesty was gracious enough to admire it and when I told Him that you had given it me He sent you His compliments upon your taste. Do not fail to send Him one as like it as possible; send it at once, by way of the Chamberlain.*") "*He need never know that in order to obtain it I had to walk into a picture. Do you remember that in the sacristy of San Martín there is a portrait by Velasquez of the Viceroy who founded the monastery and of his wife and brat? and that his wife is wearing a gold chain? I resolved that only that chain would do. So one midnight I slipped into the sacristy, climbed upon the robing-table like a girl of twelve and walked in. The canvas resisted for a moment, but the painter himself came forward to lift me through the pigment. I told him that the most beautiful girl in Spain wished to present the finest gold chain that could be found to the most gracious king in the world. It was as simple as that, and there we stood talking, we four, in the gray and silvery air that makes a Velasquez. Now I keep thinking about a more golden light; I keep looking at the Palace: I must pass the evening in a Titian. Would the Viceroy let me?*

«But His Excellency has the gout again. I say 'again' because the flattery of the court insists that there are times when he is free of it. This being Saint Mark's day His Excellency started out to visit the University where twenty-two new doctors were being brought into the world. He had hardly been carried from his divan to his coach when he screamed and refused to go any farther. He was carried back to his bed where he broke a most delicious cigar and sent for the Perichole. And while we listened to long doctrinal addresses, more or less in Latin, he heard all about us, more or less in Spanish, from the reddest and cruellest lips in town.» (Doña María permitted herself this passage, although she had just read in her daughter's last letter: *"How many times must I tell you*

to be more cautious in the things you say in your letters? They often show signs of having been opened on the journey. Nothing could be more ill-judged than your remarks on the you-know-what-I-mean at Cuzco. Such remarks are not funny, even though Vicente did compliment you upon them in his postscript, and they might get us into a great deal of trouble with Certain Persons here in Spain. I continue to be astonished that your indiscretions have not long since led to your being ordered to retire to your farm.")

«There was a great press at the Exercises and two women fell from the balcony, but God in His goodness saw that they fell on Doña Merced. All three are badly hurt, but will be thinking of other things within a year. The President was speaking at the moment of the accident and being short-sighted could not imagine what the disturbance of cries and talk and falling bodies could be about. It was very pleasant to see him bowing, under the impression that he was being applauded.

«Speaking of the Perichole, and of applause, you should know that Pepita and I decided to go to the Comedia this evening. The public still idolizes its Perichole; it even forgives her her years. We are told that she saves what she can, every morning, by passing alternate pencils of ice and fire across her cheeks.» (Translation falls especially short of this conceit which carries the whole flamboyance of the Spanish language. It was intended as an obsequious flattery of the Condesa, and was untrue. The great actress was twenty-eight at this time; her cheeks had the smoothness and polish of dark yellow marble

and would certainly have retained that quality for many years. Apart from the cosmetics required by her performances the only treatment Camila Perichole afforded her face was to throw cold water at it twice a day, like a peasant woman at a horse trough.) *"That curious man they call Uncle Pio is by her all the time. Don Rubío says that he cannot make out whether Uncle Pio is her father, her lover, or her son. The Perichole gave a wonderful performance. Scold me all you like for a provincial ninny, you have no such actresses in Spain."* And so on.

It is on this visit to the theatre that further matter hangs. She decided to go to the Comedia where the Perichole was playing Doña Leonor in Moreto's *Trampa Adelante*; perhaps some material could be derived from the visit for her daughter's next letter. She took with her Pepita, a little girl about whom later we shall learn much. Doña María had borrowed her from the orphanage connected with the Convent of Santa María Rosa de las Rosas to be her companion. The Marquesa sat in her box gazing with flagging attention at the brilliant stage. Between the acts it was the Perichole's custom to lay aside the courtly rôle and appear before the curtain to sing a few topical songs. The malicious actress had seen the Marquesa arrive and presently began improvising couplets alluding to her appearance, her avarice, her drunkenness, and even to her daughter's flight from her. The attention of the house was subtly directed to the old woman and a rising murmur of contempt accompanied the laughter of the audience. But the Marquesa, deeply moved by the first two acts of the comedy, scarcely saw the singer and sat staring before her, thinking about Spain. Camila Perichole became bolder and the air was electric with the hatred and glee of the crowd. At last Pepita plucked the Marquesa's sleeve and whispered to her that they should go. As they left the box the house arose and burst into a roar of triumph; the Perichole flung herself into a frenzied dance, for she saw the manager at the back of the hall and knew that her salary had been increased. But the Marquesa remained unaware of what had taken place; in fact she was quite pleased, for during the visit she had contrived a few felicitous phrases, phrases (who knows) that might bring a smile to her daughter's face and might make her murmur: "Really, my mother is charming."

In due time the report reached the Viceroy's ears that one of his aristocrats had been openly baited in the theatre. He summoned the Perichole to the Palace and ordered her to call upon the Marquesa and to apologize. The trip was to be made barefoot and in a black dress. Camila argued and fought, but all she gained was a pair of shoes.

The Viceroy had three reasons for insisting. In the first place the singer had taken liberties with his court. Don Andrés had contrived to make exile endurable by building up a ceremonial so complicated that it could be remembered only by a society that had nothing else to think about. He nursed his little aristocracy and its minute distinctions and any insult paid to a Marquesa was an insult to His Person. In the second place, Doña María's son-in-law was an increasingly important personage in Spain, laden with possibilities of injury to the Viceroy, nay with the possibility of supplanting him. The Conde Vicente d'Abuirre must not be vexed, even through his half-wit mother-in-law. Finally, the Viceroy was delighted to humble the actress. He suspected that she was deceiving him with a matador, perhaps with an actor,—between the flattery of the court and the inertia of gout he could not quite make out who it was; at all events, it was clear that the singer was beginning to forget that he was one of the first men in the world.

The Marquesa, beside not having heard the scurrilous songs, was in other ways unprepared for the actress's visit. You should know that after the departure of her daughter, Doña María had lighted upon a certain consolation: she had taken to drinking. Everyone drank *chicha* in Peru and there was no particular disgrace in being found unconscious on a feast day. Doña María had begun to discover that her feverish monologues had a way of keeping her awake all night. Once she took a delicate fluted glassful of *chicha* on retiring. Oblivion was so sweet that presently she stole larger amounts and tried dissimulating their effects from Pepita; she hinted that she was not well, and represented herself as going into a decline. At last she resigned all pretense. The boats that carried her letter to Spain did not leave oftener than once a month. During the week that preceded the making of the packet

she observed a strict regimen and cultivated the city assiduously for material. At last on the eve of the post she wrote the letter, making up the bundle towards dawn and leaving it for Pepita to deliver to the agent. Then as the sun rose she would shut herself up in her room with some flagons and drift through the next few weeks without the burden of consciousness. Finally she would emerge from her happiness and prepare to go into a state of "training" in preparation for the writing of another letter.

Thus on the night following the scandal in the theatre she wrote Letter XXII and retired to bed with a carafe. All next day Pepita moved about the room, glancing anxiously at the figure on the bed. The next afternoon Pepita brought her needlework into the room. The Marquesa lay staring at the ceiling with wide-open eyes, talking to herself. Towards dusk Pepita was called to the door and informed that the Perichole had come to see the mistress. Pepita remembered the theatre very well and sent back word angrily that the mistress refused to see her. The man carried the message to the street door, but returned awestruck with the news that the Señora Perichole was armed with a letter from the Viceroy presenting her to the lady. Pepita tiptoed to the bed and started talking to the Marquesa. The glazed eyes moved to the girl's face. Pepita shook her gently. With great effort Doña María tried to fix her mind on what was being said to her. Twice she lay back, refusing to seize the meaning, but at last, like a general calling together in a rain and by night the dispersed division of his army she assembled memory and attention and a few other faculties and painfully pressing her hand to her forehead she asked for a bowl of snow. When it was brought her, she long and drowsily pressed handfuls of it against her temples and cheeks; then rising she stood for a long time leaning against the bed and looking at her shoes. At last she raised her head with decision, she called for her fur-trimmed cloak and a veil. She put them on and tottered into her handsomest reception room where the actress stood waiting for her.

Camila had intended to be perfunctory and if possible impudent, but now she was struck for the first time with the dignity of the old woman. The mercer's daughter could carry herself at times with all the distinction of the Montemayors and when she was drunk she wore the grandeur of Hecuba. For Camila the half-closed eyes had the air of weary authority and she began almost timidly:

"I come, señora, to make sure that you could not have misunderstood anything I said on the evening that Your Grace did me the honour to visit my theatre."

"Misunderstood? Misunderstood?" said the Marquesa.

"Your Grace might have misunderstood and thought that my words were intended to be disrespectful to Your Grace."

"To me?"

"Your Grace is not offended at her humble servant? Your Grace is aware that a poor actress in my position may be carried beyond her intentions

... that it is very difficult ... that everything...."

"How can I be offended, señora? All that I can remember is that you gave a beautiful performance. You are a great artist. You should be happy, happy. My handkerchief, Pepita...."

The Marquesa brought out these words very rapidly and vaguely, but the Perichole was confounded. A piercing sense of shame filled her. She turned crimson. At last she was able to murmur:

"It was in the songs between the acts of the comedy. I was afraid Your Grace ..."

"Yes, yes. I remember now. I left early. Pepita, we left early, did we not? But, señora, you are good enough to forgive my leaving early, yes, even in the middle of your admirable performance. I forget why we left. Pepita ... oh, some indisposition...."

It was impossible that anyone in the theatre could have missed the intention of the songs. Camila could only assume that the Marquesa, out of a sort of fantastic magnanimity, was playing the farce of not having noticed it. She was almost in tears: "But you are so good to overlook my childishness, señora,—I mean Your Grace. I did not know. I did not know your goodness, señora, permit me to kiss your hand."

Doña María held out her hand astonished. She had not for a long time been addressed with such consideration. Her neighbors, her tradespeople, her servants—for even Pepita lived in awe of her,—her very daughter had never approached her thus. It induced a new mood in her; one that must very likely be called maudlin. She became loquacious:

"Offended, offended at you, my beautiful, ... my gifted child? Who am I, a ... an unwise and unloved old woman, to be offended at you? I felt, my daughter, as though I were—what says the poet?—*surprising through a cloud the conversation of the angels.* Your voice kept finding new wonders in our Moreto. When you said:

'*Don Juan, si mi amor estimas, Y la fe segura es necia, Enojarte mis temores Es no quererme discreta? Tan seguros....*'

and so on,—that was true! And what a gesture you made at the close of the First Day. There, with your hand so. Such a gesture as the Virgin made, saying to Gabriel: *How is it possible that I shall have a child?* No, no, you will begin to have resentment at me, for I am going to tell you about a gesture that you may remember to use some day. Yes, it would fit well into that scene where you forgive your Don Juan de Lara. Perhaps I should tell you that I saw it made one day by my daughter. My daughter is a very beautiful woman ... everyone thinks. Did ... did you know my Doña Clara, Señora?"

"Her Grace often did me the honour of visiting my theatre. I knew the Condesa well by sight."

"Do not remain so, on one knee, my child.—Pepita, tell Jenarito to bring this lady some sweet-cakes at once. Think, one day we fell out, I forget over what. Oh, there is nothing strange in that; all we mothers from time to time.... Look, can you come a little closer? You must not believe the town that says she was unkind

to me. You are a great woman with a beautiful nature and you can see further than the crowd sees in these matters.—It is a pleasure to talk to you. What beautiful hair you have! What beautiful hair!—She had not a warm impulsive nature, I know that. But, oh, my child, she has such a store of intelligence and graciousness. Any misunderstandings between us are so plainly my fault; is it not wonderful that she is so quick to forgive me? This day there fell one of those little moments. We both said hasty things and went off to our rooms. Then each turned back to be forgiven. Finally only a door separated us and there we were pulling it in contrary ways. But at last she ... took my ... face ... thus, in her two white hands. So! Look!"

The Marquesa almost fell out of her chair as she leaned forward, her face streaming with happy tears, and made the beatific gesture. I should say the mythical gesture, for the incident was but a recurring dream.

"I am glad you are here," she continued, "for now you have heard from my own lips that she is not unkind to me, as some people say. Listen, señora, the fault was mine. Look at me. Look at me. There was some mistake that made me the mother of so beautiful a girl. I am difficult. I am trying. You and she are great women. No, do not stop me: you are rare women, and I am only a nervous ... a foolish ... a stupid woman. Let me kiss your feet. I am impossible. I am impossible. I am impossible."

Here indeed the old woman did fall out of her chair and was gathered up by Pepita and led back to her bed. The Perichole walked home in consternation and sat for a long time gazing into her eyes in the mirror, her palms pressed against her cheeks.

But the person who saw most of the difficult hours of the Marquesa was her little companion, Pepita. Pepita was an orphan and had been brought up by that strange genius of Lima, the Abbess Madre María del Pilar. The only occasion upon which the two great women of Peru (as the perspective of history was to reveal them) met face to face was on the day when Doña María called upon the directress of the Convent of Santa María Rosa de las Rosas and asked if she might borrow some bright girl from the orphanage to be her companion. The Abbess gazed hard at the grotesque old woman. Even the wisest people in the world are not perfectly wise and Madre María del Pilar who was able to divine the poor human heart behind all the masks of folly and defiance, had always refused to concede one to the Marquesa de Montemayor. She asked her a great many questions and then paused to think. She wanted to give Pepita the worldly experience of living in the palace. She also wanted to bend the old woman to her own interests. And she was filled with a sombre indignation, for she knew she was gazing at one of the richest women in Peru, and the blindest.

She was one of those persons who have allowed their lives to be gnawed away because they have fallen in love with an idea several centuries before its appointed appearance in the history of civilization. She hurled herself against the obstinacy of her time in her desire to attach a little dignity to women. At midnight when she had finished adding up the accounts of the House she would fall into insane vision of an age when women could be organized to protect women, women travelling, women as servants, women when they are old or ill, the women she had discovered in the mines of Potosi, or in the workrooms of the cloth-merchants, the girls she had collected out of doorways on rainy nights. But always the next morning she had to face the fact that the women in Peru, even her nuns, went through life with two notions: one, that all the misfortunes that might befall them were merely due to the fact that they were not sufficiently attractive to bind some man to their maintenance and, two, that all the misery in the world was worth his caress. She had never known any country but the environs of Lima and she assumed that all its corruption was the normal state of mankind. Looking back from our century we can see the whole folly of her hope. Twenty such women would have failed to make any impression on that age. Yet she continued diligently in her task. She resembled the swallow in the fable who once every thousand years transferred a grain of wheat, in the hope of rearing a mountain to reach the moon. Such persons are raised up in every age; they obstinately insist on transporting their grains of wheat and they derive a certain exhilaration from the sneers of the bystanders. "How queerly they dress!" we cry. "How queerly they dress!"

Her plain red face had great kindliness, and more idealism than kindliness, and more generalship than idealism. All her work, her hospitals, her orphanage, her convent, her sudden journeys of rescue, depended upon money. No one harbored a fairer admiration for mere goodness, but she had been obliged to watch herself sacrificing her kindliness, almost her idealism, to generalship, so dreadful were the struggles to obtain her subsidies from her superiors in the church. The Archbishop of Lima, whom we shall know later in a more graceful connection, hated her with what he called a Vatinian hate and counted the cessation of her visits among the compensations for dying.

Lately she had felt not only the breath of old age against her cheek, but a graver warning. A chill of terror went through her, not for herself, but for her work. Who was there in Peru to value the things she had valued? And rising one day at dawn she had made a rapid journey through her hospital and convent and orphanage, looking for a soul she might train to be her successor. She hurried from empty face to empty face, occasionally pausing more from hope than conviction. In the courtyard she came upon a company of girls at work over the linen and her eyes fell at once upon a girl of twelve who was directing the others at the trough and at the same time recounting to them with great dramatic fire the less probable miracles in the life of Saint Rose of Lima. So it was that the search ended with Pepita. The education for greatness is difficult enough at any time, but amid the sensibilities and jealousies of a convent it must be conducted with fantastic indirection.

Pepita was assigned to the most disliked tasks in the House, but she came to understand all the aspects of its administration. She accompanied the Abbess on her journeys, even though it was in the capacity of custodian of the eggs and vegetables. And everywhere, by surprise, hours would open up in which the Directress suddenly appeared and talked to her at great length, not only on religious experience, but on how to manage women and how to plan contagious wards and how to beg for money. It was a step in this education for greatness that led to Pepita's arriving one day and entering upon the crazy duties of being Doña María's companion. For the first two years she merely came for occasional afternoons, but finally she came to the palace to live. She never had been taught to expect happiness, and the inconveniences, not to say terrors, of her new position did not seem to her excessive for a girl of fourteen. She did not suspect that the Abbess, even there, was hovering above the house, herself estimating the stresses and watching for the moment when a burden harms and not strengthens.

A few of Pepita's trials were physical: for example, the servants in the house took advantage of Doña María's indisposition; they opened up the bedrooms of the palace to their relatives; they stole freely. Alone Pepita stood out against them and suffered a persecution of small discomforts and practical jokes. Her mind, similarly, had its distresses: when she accompanied Doña María on her errands in the city, the older woman would be seized with the desire to dash into a church, for what she had lost of religion as faith she had replaced with religion as magic. "Stay here in the sunlight, my dear child; I shall not be long," she would say. Doña María would then forget herself in a reverie before the altar and leave the church by another door. Pepita had been brought up by Madre María del Pilar to an almost morbid obedience and when after many hours she ventured into the church and made sure that her mistress was no longer there, still she returned to the street-corner and waited while the shadows fell gradually across the square. Thus waiting in public she suffered all the torture of a little girl's self-consciousness. She still wore the uniform of the orphanage (which a minute's thoughtfulness on the part of Doña María could have altered) and she suffered hallucinations wherein men seemed to be staring at her and whispering—nor were these always hallucinations. No less her heart suffered, for on some days Doña María would suddenly become aware of her and would talk to her cordially and humorously, would let appear for a few hours all the exquisite sensibility of the Letters; then, on the morrow she would withdraw into herself again and, while never harsh, would become impersonal and unseeing. The beginnings of hope and affection that Pepita had such need to expend would be wounded. She tiptoed about the palace, silent, bewildered, clinging only to her sense of duty and her loyalty to her "mother in the Lord," Madre María del Pilar, who had sent her there.

FINALLY A NEW FACT APPEARED THAT was to have considerable effect on the lives of both the Marquesa and her companion: "*My dear mother,*" wrote the Condesa, "*the weather has been most exhausting and the fact that the orchards and gardens are in bloom only makes it the more trying. I could endure flowers if only they had no perfume. I shall therefore ask your permission to write you at less length than usual. If Vicente returns before the post leaves he will be delighted to finish out the leaf and supply you with those tiresome details about myself which you seem to enjoy so. I shall not go to Grignan in Provence as I expected this Fall, as child will be born in early October.*"

What child? The Marquesa leaned against the wall. Doña Clara had foreseen the exhausting importunities that this news would waken in her mother and had sought to mitigate them by the casualness of her announcement. The ruse did not succeed. The famous Letter XLII was the answer.

Now at length the Marquesa had something to be anxious about: her daughter was to become a mother. This event, which merely bored Doña Clara, discovered a whole new scale of emotions in the Marquesa. She became a mine of medical knowledge and suggestion. She combed the city for wise old women and poured into her letters the whole folk-wisdom of the New World. She fell into the most abominable superstition. She practiced a degrading system of taboos for her child's protection. She refused to allow a knot in the house. The maids were forbidden to tie up their hair and she concealed upon her person ridiculous symbols of a happy delivery. On the stairs the even steps were marked with red chalk and a maid who accidentally stepped upon an even step was driven from the house with tears and screams. Doña Clara was in the hands of malignant Nature who reserves the right to inflict upon her children the most terrifying jests. There was an etiquette of propitiation which generations of peasant women had found comforting. So vast an army of witnesses surely implied that there was some truth in it. At least it could do no harm, and Perhaps it did good. But the Marquesa did not only satisfy the rites of paganism; she studied the prescriptions of Christianity as well. She arose in the dark and stumbled through the streets to the earliest Masses. She hysterically hugged the altar-rails trying to rend from the gaudy statuettes a sign, only a sign, the ghost of a smile, the furtive nod of a waxen head. Would all be well? Sweet, sweet Mother, would all be well?

At times, after a day's frantic resort to such invocations, a revulsion would sweep over her. Nature is deaf. God is indifferent. Nothing in man's power can alter the course of law. Then on some street-corner she would stop, dizzy with despair, and leaning against a wall would long to be taken from a world that had no plan in it. But soon a belief in the great Perhaps would surge up from the depths of her nature and she would fairly run home to renew the candles above her daughter's bed.

At last the time came to satisfy the supreme rite of Peruvian households looking forward to this event: she made the pilgrimage to the shrine of Santa María de Cluxambuqua. If there resided any efficacy in devotion at all, surely it lay in a visit to this great shrine. The ground had been holy through three religions; even before the Incan civilization distraught human beings had hugged the rocks and lashed themselves with whips to wring their will from the skies. Thither the Marquesa was carried in her chair, crossing the bridge of San Luis Rey and ascending up into the hills toward that city of large-girdled women, a tranquil town, slow-moving and slow-smiling; a city of crystal air, cold as the springs that fed its many fountains; a city of bells, soft and musical, and tuned to carry on with one another the happiest quarrels. If anything turned out for disappointment in the town of Cluxambuqua the grief was somehow assimilated by the overwhelming immanence of the Andes and by the weather of quiet joy that flowed in and about the side-streets. No sooner did the Marquesa see from a distance the white walls of this town perched on the knees of the highest peaks than her fingers ceased turning the beads and the busy prayers of her fright were cut short on her lips.

She did not even alight at the inn, but leaving Pepita to arrange for their stay she went on to the church and knelt for a long time patting her hands softly together. She was listening to the new tide of resignation that was rising within her. Perhaps she would learn in time to permit both her daughter and her gods to govern their own affairs. She was not annoyed by the whispering of the old women in padded garments who sold candles and medals and talked about money from dawn to dark. She was not even distracted by an officious sacristan who tried to collect a fee for something or other and who, from spite, made her change her place under the pretext of repairing a tile on the floor. Presently she went out into the sunshine and sat on the steps of the fountain. She watched the little processions of invalids slowly revolving about the gardens. She watched three hawks plunging about the sky. The children who had been playing by the fountain stared at her for a moment, and went away alarmed, but a llama (a lady with a long neck and sweet shallow eyes, burdened down by a fur cape too heavy for her and picking her way delicately down an interminable staircase) came over and offered her a velvet cleft nose to stroke. The llama is deeply interested in the men about her, is even fond of pretending that she too is one of them and of inserting her head into their conversations as though in a moment she would lift her voice and contribute a wan and helpful comment. Soon Doña María was surrounded by a number of these sisters who seemed on the point of asking her why she clapped her hands so and how much her veiling cost a yard.

Doña María had arranged that any letters arriving from Spain should be brought to her at once by a special messenger. She had travelled slowly from Lima and even now as she sat in the square a boy from her farm ran up and put into her hand a large packet wrapped in parchment and dangling some nuggets of sealing-wax. Slowly she undid the wrappings. With measured stoic gestures she read first an affectionate and jocose note from her son-in-law; then her daughter's letter. It was full of wounding remarks rather brilliantly said, perhaps said for the sheer virtuosity of giving pain neatly. Each of its phrases found its way through the eyes of the Marquesa, then, carefully wrapped in understanding and forgiveness it sank into her heart. At last she arose, gently dispersed the sympathetic llamas, and with a grave face returned to the shrine.

While Doña María was passing the late afternoon in the Church and in the Square, Pepita was left to prepare their lodging. She showed the porters where to lay down the great wicker hampers and set about unpacking the altar, the brazier, the tapestries and the portraits of Doña Clara. She descended into the kitchen and gave the cook exact instructions as to the preparations of a certain porridge upon which the Marquesa principally subsisted. Then she returned to the rooms and waited. She resolved to write a letter to the Abbess. She hung for a long time over the quill, staring into the distance with trembling lip. She saw the face of Madre María del Pilar, so red and scrubbed, and the wonderful black eyes. She heard her voice as at the close of supper (the orphans sitting with lowered eyes and folded hands) she commented on the events of the day, or as, by candlelight, she stood among the beds of the hospital and announced the theme for meditation during the night. But most clearly of all Pepita remembered the sudden interviews when the Abbess (not daring to wait until the girl was older) had discussed with her the duties of her office. She had talked to Pepita as to an equal. Such speech is troubling and wonderful to an intelligent child and Madre María del Pilar had abused it. She had expanded Pepita's vision of how she should feel and act beyond the measure of her years. And she had unthinkingly turned upon Pepita the full blaze of her personality, as Jupiter had turned his upon Semele. Pepita was frightened by her sense of insufficiency; she hid it and wept. And then the Abbess had cast the child into the discipline of this long solitude, where Pepita struggled, refusing to let herself believe that she had been abandoned. And now from this strange inn in these strange mountains, where the altitude was making her lightheaded, Pepita longed for the dear presence, the only real thing in her life.

She wrote a letter, all inkstains and incoherence. Then she went downstairs to see about fresh charcoal and to taste the porridge.

The Marquesa came in and sat down at the table. "I can do no more. What will be, will be," she whispered. She unbound from her neck the amulets of her superstition and dropped them into the glowing brazier. She had a strange sense of having antagonized God by too much prayer and so addressed Him now obliquely. "After all it is in the hands of another. I no longer claim the least influence. What

will be, will be." She sat for a long time, her palms against her cheeks, making a blank of her mind. Her eyes fell on Pepita's letter. She opened it mechanically and started to read. She had read a full half of it before her attention was aware of the meaning of the words: "... *but all this is nothing if you like me and wish me to stay with her. I oughtn't to tell you but every now and then the bad chambermaids lock me up in rooms and steal things and perhaps My Lady will think that I steal them. I hope not. I hope you are well and not having any trouble in the hospital or anywhere. Though I never see you I think of you all the time and I remember what you told me, my dear mother in God. I want to do only what you want, but if you could let me come back for a few days to the convent, but not if you do not wish it. But I am so much alone and not talking to anyone, and everything. Sometimes I do not know whether you have forgotten me and if you could find a minute to write me a little letter or something, I could keep it, but I know how busy you are...."*

Doña María read no further. She folded the letter and put it aside. For a moment she was filled with envy: she longed to command another's soul as completely as this nun was able to do. Most of all she longed to be back in this simplicity of love, to throw off the burden of pride and vanity that hers had always carried. To quiet the tumult in her mind she picked up a book of devotion and tried to fix her attention upon the words. But after a moment she suddenly felt the need to reread the whole letter, to surprise, if possible, the secret of so much felicity.

Pepita returned bringing the supper in her hands, followed by a maid. Doña María watched her over the top of her book as she would have watched a visitor from Heaven. Pepita tiptoed about the room laying the table and whispering directions to her assistant.

"Your supper is ready, My Lady," she said at last.

"But, my child, you are going to eat with me?" In Lima Pepita generally sat down at the table with her mistress.

"I thought you would be tired, My Lady. I had my supper downstairs."

"She does not wish to eat with me," thought the Marquesa. "She knows me and has rejected me."

"Would you like me to read aloud to you while you are eating, My Lady?" asked Pepita, who felt that she had made a mistake.

"No. You may go to bed, if you choose."

"Thank you, My Lady."

Doña María had risen and approached the table. With one hand on the back of the chair she said haltingly: "My dear child, I am sending off a letter to Lima in the morning. If you have one you can enclose it with mine."

"No, I have none," said Pepita. She added hastily: "I must go downstairs and get you the new charcoal."

"But, my dear, you have one for ... Madre María del Pilar. Wouldn't you?"

Pepita pretended to be busy over the brazier. "No, I'm not going to send it," she said. She was aware during the long pause that followed that the Marquesa was staring at her in stupefaction. "I've changed my mind."

"I know she would like a letter from you, Pepita. It would make her very happy. I know."

Pepita was reddening. She said loudly: "The innkeeper said that there would be some new charcoal ready for you at dark. I'll tell them to bring it up now." She glanced hastily at the old woman and saw that she had not ceased from staring at her with great sad inquiring eyes. Pepita felt that these were not things one talked about, but the strange woman seemed to be feeling the matter so strongly that Pepita was willing to concede one more answer: "No, it was a bad letter. It wasn't a good letter."

Doña María fairly gasped. "Why, my dear Pepita, I think it was very beautiful. Believe me, I know. No, no; what could have made it a bad letter?"

Pepita frowned, hunting for a word that would close the matter.

"It wasn't ... it wasn't ... brave," she said. And then she would say no more. She carried the letter off into her own room and could be heard tearing it up. Then she got into bed and lay staring into the darkness, still uncomfortable at having talked in such a fashion. And Doña María sat down to her dish amazed.

She had never brought courage to either life or love. Her eyes ransacked her heart. She thought of the amulets and of her beads, her drunkenness ... she thought of her daughter. She remembered the long relationship, crowded with the wreckage of exhumed conversations, of fancied slights, of inopportune confidences, of charges of neglect and exclusion (but she must have been mad that day; she remembered beating upon the table). "But it's not my fault," she cried. "It's not my fault that I was so. It was circumstance. It was the way I was brought up. Tomorrow I begin a new life. Wait and see, oh my child." At I last she cleared away the table and sitting down wrote what she called her first letter, her first stumbling misspelled letter in courage. She remembered with shame that in the previous one she had piteously asked her daughter how much she loved her, and had greedily quoted the few and hesitant endearments that Doña Clara had lately ventured to her. Doña María could not recall those pages, but she could write some new ones, free and generous. No one else has regarded them as stumbling. It is the famous letter LVI, known to the Encyclopedists as her Second Corinthians because of its immortal paragraph about love: "Of the thousands of persons we meet in a lifetime, my child ..." and so on. It was almost dawn when she finished the letter. She opened the door upon her balcony and looked at the great tiers of stars that glittered above the Andes. Throughout the hours of the night, though there had been few to hear it, the whole sky had been loud with the singing of these constellations. Then she took a candle into the next room and looked at Pepita as she slept, and pushed back the damp hair from the girl's face. "Let me live now," she whispered. "Let me begin again."

Two days later they started back to Lima, and while crossing the bridge of San Luis Rey the accident which we know befell them.

TO BE CONTINUED IN
LITERARY OUTLAW #2

GONE

(for John and June)

the cowboys have died, one by one, the horses,
the longhorn and bar x. the hobo and outlaw,
the hippies,
the poets, writers,
the singers, the actors,
day by day have crept off the stage.
they left us grainy black and white movies,
phantom woods, village squares, tumbleweed,
decrying of the gun, the passage of lava lamps,
the echo of rail song wailing out the dark of night,
pale community center reproduction of masterpieces,

we are overflowing with the words they left behind
in gravel voice or lonely act or scratched mark.
sometimes we have the sound of words,
their shape as defined in one lone act,
or their direction in a movement.
what they could never capture
and what we carry
truer than dvd
are the memories
of a moment, a tune, a word, and idea.
gone they are but gone they'll never be.

—Patty Summers
12 September 2003

Edgar Allan Poe's BERENICE

WRITTEN BY EDGAR ALLAN POE

ILLUSTRATED BY RICARDO VILLAMONTE

...ABOUT A MONTH AGO, ONLY A MONTH AGO, BERENICE FELL ILL HORRIBLY ILL, AND BEGAN SLOWLY TO CHANGE...
...DISEASE... FATAL DISEASE-- FELL UPON HER ...EVEN AS I LOOKED UPON HER SHE CHANGED... NO LONGER HIGH SPIRITED...NO LONGER BEAUTIFUL.
...WHEN WE WERE YOUNG...AND WHEN SHE WAS BEAUTIFUL, I DID NOT LOVE HER...NOW AS SHE BECAME ILL, AND ALMOST FEARSOME TO LOOK UPON-- I FELL DEEPLY IN LOVE WITH HER... IT WAS MY DISEASE THAT MADE ME LOVE HER OF COURSE...IT WAS WHEN I SHUDDERED TO LOOK AT HER, THAT I CAME TO LOVE HER...
...I LOVE YOU, BERENICE...WITH ALL MY HEART... MARRY ME...
OH, YES EGAEUS... I WILL...
...AND IN THE MONTHS BEFORE OUR MARRIAGE-- SHE BECAME DETERIO-RATED...AND I BECAME MORE MOROSE THAN EVER...

...ONE NIGHT...AS BERENICE AND I SAT IN MY LIBRARY...I LOOKED AT HER...LOOKED AT HER THROUGH MY DISEASED EYES...AS I HAD NEVER SEEN HER BEFORE...
...SHE SPOKE NO WORD, BUT AN ICY CHILL RAN THROUGH MY BODY AS MY EYES WERE RIVETED UPON HER...
...HER EMACIATION WAS GROTESQUE...HER ARMS WERE AS THIN AS STICKS...
...HER HAIR HAD BECOME YELLOW AND RUINED...
...THE EYES WERE WITHOUT LIFE...
...HER TEETH...HER TEETH...OH, GOD, THEY WERE ROTTED IN HER MOUTH...
...SHE LEFT ME ALONE...BUT STILL I THOUGHT OF THE TEETH...BECAUSE OF MY ILLNESS I COULD NOT GET THEM OUT OF MY MIND...

...THEN CAME THE FULL FURY OF MY MONOMANIA... I STRUGGLED AGAINST IT IN VAIN... I COULD NOT GET HER TEETH OUT OF MY MIND...
...I VISUALIZED THEM IN MY MIND'S EYE... TEETH...
...I OBSERVED THEM IN MY MIND FROM EVERY ANGLE...FROM EVERY POINT OF VIEW...THOSE TEETH... I WAS POSSESSED...BY THOSE TEETH...
...I SAT LIKE THAT SEVERAL HOURS...WITHOUT MOVING TILL A SERVANT-GIRL ENTERED THE LIBRARY WEEPING...
...SHE IS DEAD...
THE MISTRESS BERENICE HAS DIED...
OH, GOD... HAVE MERCY ON HER SOUL...HAVE MERCY ON MY SOUL...HAVE MERCY, GOD...

...SHE HAD BEEN SEIZED BY EPILEPSY AND HAD FAINTED-DEAD IN THE SIGHT OF THE SERVANT-GIRL...
...WE BURIED BERENICE IN THE FAMILY PLOT IN THE CASTLE GROUNDS THE FOLLOWING DAY...
...I THEN WENT TO THE LIBRARY-- AND DID NOT LEAVE FOR SEVERAL DAYS... ALL THE TIME I MERELY THOUGHT OF HER...AND OF HER TEETH... OF HER TEETH THAT POSSESSED ME...
SIR...SIR... WAKE UP...THE GRAVE SIR...IT HAS BEEN VIOLATED...
...YOU SAY THERE WAS A WILD CRY IN THE NIGHT...AND THE GRAVE HAS BEEN VIOLATED?
BUT THAT'S NOT ALL SIR... THE POSITION OF HER BODY...THE LOOK ABOUT HER FACE...INDICATES MISTRESS BERENICE WAS NOT DEAD WHEN SHE WAS BURIED!
WHAT? OH...I MUST HAVE BEEN ASLEEP...WHAT IS IT? WHAT IS WRONG?

NOT...DEAD? SHE WAS BURIED PREMATURELY?
YOUR CLOTHES, SIR...
...MY CLOTHES? WHAT ABOUT THEM?
MY HANDS... MY FINGERNAILS CLOTTED WITH BLOOD!
...THEY ARE FILTHY WITH MUD...GORE... BLOOD IS ALL OVER YOU...
OH, GOD, NO!!
WHAT IS THIS, SIR?
WHAT IS THIS LITTLE BOX SIR?
WHAT HAVE I DONE!!
...A SHOVEL... ...YOU'VE BEEN DIGGING!
...WITH A SHRIEK I FELL TO THE FLOOR LOOKING AT THE BOX...

...IT WAS OBVIOUS...
...WHAT I HAD DONE...
...I REALIZED...
...WHEN I HELD UP THE HEAD OF BERENICE...
...I DROPPED THE BOX...IT FELL FROM MY HANDS...
...IT BURST INTO PIECES ON THE FLOOR...AND FALLING OUT OF IT, WERE SOME INSTRUMENTS OF DENTAL SURGERY, AND THIRTY-TWO WHITE AND IVORY-LOOKING SUBSTANCES THAT SCATTERED TO AND FRO ABOUT THE FLOOR...

CONTRIBUTORS

ROBERT W. CHAMBERS (1865 – 1933) was an American artist and fiction writer, best known for his book of short stories titled *The King in Yellow*.

JOHN GRAVES publishes Literary Outlaw magazine and hosts the Literary Outlaw podcast. He lives on a working farm in the shadow of the Blue Ridge Mountains in Virginia. He's half southern, half yankee, and all American. He describes himself as an Ecclesiastes 1:17 man married to a Proverbs 31 woman. John is the author of the *Starship Gilead* trilogy and the forthcoming weird western series *Rook: God's Gunslinger*.

EDGAR ALLAN POE (1809 – 1849) was an American writer, poet, author, editor, and literary critic who is best known for his poetry and short stories, particularly his tales of mystery and the macabre.

KEVIN G. SUMMERS is the author of *Legendarium*, *The Man Who Shot John Wilkes Booth*, and *The Bleak December*.

PATTY SUMMERS (1947 – 2012) lived in Stratford, New Hampshire. She was the editor of the literary magazine, *Phoebe*, and wrote several novels, including *Sugarloaf* and *The Brunswick Journals*.

KURT VONNEGUT JR. (1922 – 2007) was an American writer and humorist known for his satirical and darkly humorous novels, most notably *Slaughterhouse Five* and *Breakfast of Champions*.

THORNTON WILDER (1897 – 1975) was an American playwright and novelist. He won three Pulitzer Prizes for the novel *The Bridge of San Luis Rey* and for the plays *Our Town* and *The Skin of Our Teeth*.

www.ingramcontent.com/pod-product-compliance
Lightning Source LLC
Chambersburg PA
CBHW060516120726
48002CB00011B/3187